Murder
by the
Book

Debbie Young

Copyright Information

MURDER BY THE BOOK
by Debbie Young

ISBN (paperback) 978-1-911223-26-9
ISBN (ebook) 978-1-911223-25-2

About the Author

Debbie Young writes warm, witty, feel-good fiction.

Her Sophie Sayers Village Mystery series of seven novels runs the course of a year in the fictional Cotswold village of Wendlebury Barrow.

Her humorous short stories are available in themed collections, such as *Marry in Haste*, *Quick Change* and *Stocking Fillers*, and in many anthologies.

She is a frequent speaker at literature festivals and writers' events, and is founder and director of the free Hawkesbury Upton Literature Festival.

A regular contributor to two local community magazines, the award-winning *Tetbury Advertiser* and the *Hawkesbury Parish News*, she has published two collections of her columns, *Young by Name* and *All Part of the Charm*. These publications offer insight into her own life in a small Cotswold village where she lives with her Scottish husband and their teenage daughter.

*For the latest information about Debbie's
books and events, visit her Writing Life website,
where you may also like to join her free Readers' Club:*
www.authordebbieyoung.com

**To Belinda Pollard,
for sharing her wisdom, humour and friendship
from the other side of the world**

"*I once sent a dozen of my friends a telegram saying, 'flee at once —
all is discovered.' They all left town immediately.*"
Mark Twain

"*When someone starts turning you into someone you are not,
that's the time you ought to say goodbye to them for good.*"
Sophie Sayers

Murder
by the
Book

1 Ding Dong Dell, Who is in the Well?

In the frosty shadows behind The Bluebird, close to the ancient well, a dark figure stumbled across the cobbles, bumping into the empty aluminium beer kegs awaiting collection by the brewery. Just then, another person emerged purposefully from the pub's side exit and stalked down the narrow passage that led to the courtyard. A halo of light spilled into the darkness, but didn't quite reach the low stone wall surrounding the well.

The two figures converged beside the well, conversing with increasing animation, until the second raised strong hands to administer a sturdy thump to the first one's chest.

Had the pub not been so full this Valentine's Night, someone inside would surely have heard the shouting and swearing. Had the night not been so chilly, the stay-at-homes might have been walking their dogs nearby, or standing at their back doors to call their cats in, or opening their kitchen windows to admit some fresh spring air.

But as it was, no-one heard the second figure curse as he turned on his heel and march smartly back to the pub door. No-one heard the shout of surprise as the first figure spilled over backwards, legs in the air, to tumble down into the dark round hole in the ground, the low wall sending a shoe flying across the yard. No-one caught the blunt thud as a head struck the side of the well, silencing any further cries of protest or shouts for help. No-one noticed the unusually loud splash, which created a much greater wake than when young Tommy Crowe, for want of anything better to do after school, chucked pebbles and sticks and stones down the well to hear the echo.

There'd be no more sounds in the courtyard until next morning, when the builder's lorry full of concrete was due to fill and seal the well as the first step in its transformation into a smart new beer garden. It would be the end of an era. The well would echo no more.

2 The Game's Afoot

From the other side of the bookshop, Tommy peered at me through his new magnifying glass, his right eye distorted by the lens.

"My mum bought me this for Christmas, to go with the book that my little sister chose for me, a junior detective's handbook. My gran gave me a detective board game she used to play when she was little."

His mother's thoughtful choice of present sent her up in my estimation. All I'd learned about her in the six months I'd lived in the village was that she was fond of wine, and thought Tommy, in his early teens, too old for Advent calendars. You are never too old for an Advent calendar. Although it was now 3 January, and I'm twenty-five, I still hadn't been able to bring myself to throw mine away.

"What have you detected so far?" I asked with an encouraging smile.

"It was Miss Scarlett in the library with the candlestick," he said.

"And in the real world?" Standing behind the tearoom counter, I was struggling to open a fresh jar of jam.

"Ooh, loads of things." He turned his magnifying glass on the old man in wellies who was tucking into a large slice of buttered toast at one of the tearoom tables. "Like Billy had eggs for breakfast this morning."

You didn't need a magnifying glass to spot the yolk congealed on the lapel of the old man's sagging jacket. Billy looked down at his chest, peeled the bright yellow lump off the grey tweed, and popped it in his mouth.

"Yuk," said Tommy, crossing over to turn his glass on a spider crawling up the window of the front door. He pulled an empty matchbox from his Parka pocket and gently inserted the spider.

I called across to the trade counter. "Hector, could you please open this jar of jam for me? The lid's stuck."

I held it up to show him. Although my arm muscles had definitely got stronger since I'd started work at the shop, what with lifting so many boxes of books every day, they weren't a patch on Hector's. I had been sorry when the weather turned chilly back in November and he'd swapped his t-shirts for long-sleeved sweaters.

Billy put out a hand to stop me as I went to take the jar to Hector, his grip surprisingly strong for a man of his age. I supposed that was down to his part-time job as village gravedigger. Oh, and jobbing gardener for the vicar. A village the size of Wendlebury Barrow doesn't need many graves.

"I'll take care of that for you, girlie," said Billy, popping the top off effortlessly. Previously I'd have thought I'd be favourite to win an arm-wrestling match against him, but now I was not so sure.

Tommy, pocketing his matchbox, returned to the tearoom and jumped up to sit on the counter. So much for health and safety.

"I also deduce that you've just come back from Inverness." Considering my travelling bags, with airline labels attached, were in full view behind the counter – Hector had collected me from the airport at 7am and brought me straight to the shop so we could open on time – Tommy's observation hardly rated as ace detective work.

"In a mess?" said Billy. "Who's in a mess?"

"Inverness, Billy," I said loudly, prompting him to adjust his hearing aids.

Tommy jumped down from the counter and crossed over to the central display table and held the magnifying glass over a pile of books.

"I could tell you who has touched these books, if you wanted me to. That is, once I've fingerprinted the whole village."

He pulled a black inkpad and a small pocket diary out of his Parka. "I had these in my Christmas stocking." He opened the diary to show me the first week of January displayed across two pages. "I'm using it to collect fingerprints and to note down clues. See, the dates are on there already, so that'll save time whenever I find new evidence."

Already the first few pages were covered in scribbled notes. Wanting to encourage Tommy in such a constructive new hobby, I turned to Billy, who was now licking his fingers to pick up the remaining toast crumbs from the table.

"Like to volunteer to be Tommy's first victim, Billy? I mean, suspect?"

Billy held up his sticky hands. "You don't need to waste your ink on me, Tom. You can have my fingerprints in raspberry jam."

Before Tommy could reply, Hector coughed. "I'd prefer not to have fingerprints of any kind taken in here, thank you very much. I don't want grubby marks on my stock."

Tommy's head jerked round in Hector's direction. "Why, have you got something to hide?" He sounded hopeful. Picking up a Hermione Minty novel, he held it up to the light to examine its glossy paper cover for traces of previous browsers.

Hector flashed me a cautious look. Only he and I knew that Hermione Minty was his pseudonym. For years he'd been writing romantic novels under her name to subsidise his income as a bookseller. As I was his girlfriend as well as his employee, he knew his secret was safe with me.

Hector's answer was truthful while evading the facts. "My conscience is clear, thank you very much. If it's local villains you're after, I suggest you look elsewhere."

"But not at me," I said quickly, as Tommy turned his magnifying glass on me. I pointed to myself with both hands. "Nothing to see here."

As if considering whether to disagree, Tommy looked me up and down, his gaze lingering longer than was comfortable for me. Half man, half boy, he was quite unlike the village schoolchildren who came to me for reading lessons in the shop after school.

"Maybe not, miss. But my mum reckons there are plenty of crimes committed in the village that never get detected. My new year's resolution is to track them all down and solve them."

"What made her say that?" asked Hector.

Billy put down his teacup with a clatter.

"You was born and raised here, Hector," he said. "Do you really have to ask?"

Hector came out from behind the counter to restore the display table to order after Tommy's inspection.

"I'd have thought the opposite was true. We've had more than our fair share of detected crimes here lately. Are you suggesting we've missed a few?"

Billy plunged his hands into his jacket pockets and pulled them out again, an action which I guessed was meant to wipe off the excess jam. "I don't mean just lately. Do you mean to tell me you never got away with any mischief when you was a lad?"

Hector moved over to the window to straighten up a crooked diet book. "I hardly ever did anything naughty in the first place, because I knew I wouldn't get away with it. Not when every grown-up in the village knew who I was, who my parents were, and where we lived."

I could imagine the orderly, fair-minded Hector as a law-abiding little boy.

"Ah, but it depends who caught you in the act," said Billy. "Supposing it was someone who liked you so much they wouldn't rat on you?"

"Good point, Billy," said Tommy, coming over to join Billy at his tea table. "If your mum knew you'd done something naughty, even if she told you off, she wouldn't shop you to the police. If she loved you, she'd take your side."

My friend Ella Berry, who works in the village school office, had told me that the teachers' complaints about Tommy's behaviour had always rolled off his mum like raindrops off an umbrella.

I laughed. "Are you suggesting Hector's mother doesn't love him?" Then, remembering I hadn't met her yet and hoping I hadn't made a terrible gaffe, I hurried to change the subject. "Covering up for a naughty child is one thing, but the law's the law."

Hector gave a lopsided smile. "Does this mean you're going to shop me for breaking the speed limit on the way back from the airport this morning?" An alarm on Hector's Land Rover, set to beep when he went over 70mph, had sounded only once on our journey that morning, on an empty downhill section of road. He'd quickly braked.

"That was only a momentary lapse of concentration," I said. "It's not like committing murder."

"It could have been murder," said Tommy, getting out his diary and his pen to note it down. "They said in the road safety film they showed us at school that speeding is a murder waiting to happen. Supposing a child had stepped out in front of you?"

"On the motorway?" I asked. "That seems unlikely."

"Why not? I've walked across a motorway before," said Tommy. "You could have murdered me."

I shuddered. Self-preservation wasn't Tommy's long suit. He had no sense of danger, as his exploits often proved. I still hadn't got over him jumping off the village hall roof during a nativity play rehearsal.

"Are you sure they didn't call it an accident waiting to happen, rather than a murder?" I said hastily.

Tommy shrugged. "Same difference. But if you killed someone on purpose, I'd have to turn you in."

"Would you, though?" Billy narrowed his eyes. "I once had a ferret who killed all her own kits when she felt threatened by a stray ferret in my garden. But I couldn't be cross with her, because that's what ferrets do. She was following her instinct. Same as they do when you take

8

them out rabbiting. They're not murderers. They're just being ferrets."

"That's a funny way of defending babies." Tommy frowned. "My mum would never do a thing like that."

"Your mum's not a ferret," I said. "But I bet if she ever thought you were in danger, she would do all she could to protect you."

"Most mothers would kill to protect their young if their lives were at stake," said Hector. "It's only natural. But not many kill their own babies."

"No, but a lot of male animals do," said Billy.

I was anxious to steer the conversation on to less sensitive territory, because Tommy's father had abandoned the family when Tommy was a small boy, leaving Tommy, his sister and his mother with a still festering sense of loss and anger.

"Thank goodness we're not animals, eh?" I said brightly.

But Billy steamrollered on. "Still, there's the law, and then there's natural law. In Wendlebury we've got our natural sense of decency on our side. We don't need any of them cameras on every street corner watching our every move like they do in them big cities. We don't need nor want Big Brother here."

Hector spluttered. "Good grief, Billy, you're making us sound like something out of *Deliverance*. Don't forget we do have our own resident policeman."

"Yes, but Bob only lives here, off duty. He doesn't patrol the streets. It's not the same as in the old days, when we had a village officer on the beat."

Tommy glanced up from his diary. "Has ferret got one r or two?"

"Two," I said. "And no i's."

He stared at me, incredulous. "No eyes? How could it see the other ferret?"

Billy ignored his interruption. "At the end of the day, what you gets up to is between you and the Almighty." It was easy to forget that beneath his shabby outer shell lay the solid faith that underpinned his role of churchwarden.

Hector took this as a cue to terminate the conversation. "So we haven't got Big Brother, but we have got God. Well, that's all right then. All's well that ends well."

His atheist's cynicism was lost on Billy.

"That's it," said Billy stoutly. "And I know which one I'd rather have preside over me in judgement."

"I've got no choice," said Tommy, closing his diary and stuffing it back in his pocket. "I haven't got a big brother. I just am one, to Sina. Maybe that's why my instinct is to watch over people."

I saw Hector glance for a moment at our set of George Orwell paperbacks. I didn't think Tommy was ready yet to tackle *1984,* a book I'd read on Hector's recommendation over the Christmas holidays.

"You don't know how lucky you are," said Billy, half to himself.

Tommy wouldn't have known the shameful history of Billy's elder brother, Bertie, and nor would I if Hector had not confided in me about it before Christmas. Bertie had run off many years before with Carol Barker, now the village shopkeeper, only to abandon her after a matter of weeks, leaving her pregnant. The baby had been taken into care by social services. Carol, like me and Hector, was an only child. What her parents must have suffered in her absence I could only imagine.

Fortunately, Tommy paid no attention to Billy's last comment, steering the conversation back to his new obsession.

"Here's one thing I've discovered since I got my detective skills book," he said. "Even the most innocent-looking people have secrets to hide. For example, I can tell you that Hector is very pleased that you've just come back from Scotland."

Hector let out a bark of laughter. "I hope you don't need your magnifying glass to see that," he said tartly. Billy sniggered.

Tommy leaned forward so that his elbows rocked the full cream jug that I'd placed on Billy's table. "Anyway, the thing is, if anybody round here has got any secrets, I'm going to find them out. I'll be an expert detective soon. I'm picking up new tips every day – how to see through disguises, how to read body language that shows when someone's guilty, how to recognise criminals from their handwriting…"

Very quietly, Hector started to remove from the display table the few remaining copies of Hermione Minty's novels that I'd persuaded him to autograph with her name in the run-up to Christmas. I'd sold one of the signed copies to Tommy to give to his mum as a Christmas present. Thinking a distraction might be a good idea for all concerned, I delved into my handbag and pulled out two small caramel-coloured bars of Scottish confectionery wrapped in clear cellophane.

"Here you go, Tommy, Billy," I said, handing them one each. "I brought you back some Scottish tablet."

Tommy pulled a face, turning it over in his hands. "Tablets? I'll never be able to swallow a tablet that size."

I laughed.

"Not tablets, Tommy, tablet," I said. "It's a famous Scottish sweet. A bit like fudge, only crumblier and tastier."

Tommy perked up. "Thanks very much, miss. I love fudge."

He peeled back the wrapper and took an enormous bite. I hoped it wouldn't trigger a sugar rush. He was hard enough work sugar-free. "Didn't you get Hector a tablet?" he asked with his mouth full.

I shook my head. "I've already given him a different present."

Billy chortled. "You didn't waste any time, girlie."

Hector put his hands to the ends of the piece of cashmere draped around his neck.

"A tartan scarf, Billy. Sophie brought me back this piece of Munro tartan. Only people whose surname is Munro, like me, have the right to wear it. It's a clan thing apparently."

As the daughter of a university lecturer in Scottish cultural history, I knew that was a myth invented in the nineteenth century, pandering to Queen Victoria's enthusiasm for all things Scottish, but I didn't bother to put him right. I was just glad he liked it.

"Cool," said Tommy politely, though I could tell he thought he'd got the better deal with his tablet.

A creak at the entrance announced the arrival of Tommy's little sister, Sina. The damp weather had made the wooden doorframe swell, and she needed to put her whole bodyweight behind the door to open it. Now she stood on the threshold, a long rope, possibly a discarded washing line, swinging from her hands.

Hector appraised her. "Sina Crowe, in the bookshop, with a skipping rope."

Sina, on a mission, ignored him. "Tommy, Mum says you've got to come home for lunch now." Her voice, high and light, belied her forceful character.

Tommy stared at her in surprise. "How did you know I was here?"

Without answering, she left as abruptly as she had arrived, yanking the door closed behind her. Waiting for Tommy to follow, she started skipping on the pavement outside the shop window, jumping steadily and gracefully over the swinging rope as she chanted aloud:

"Ding, dong, dell,
Pussy's in the well,
Who threw her in?
Little Tommy Crowe…"

Tommy frowned. "I'll throw Little Sina Crowe down the well if she doesn't look out. That doesn't even rhyme." Stuffing the rest of the tablet in his pocket, he headed for the door, turning back to speak to us over his shoulder before he left. "I think she must have been reading my detective book. I'll dust it for fingerprints as soon as I get home with the talcum powder my gran gave Mum for Christmas. I'll make Wendlebury Barrow a safer place before long, don't you worry."

With the strength of a man and the enthusiasm of a boy, he slammed the door shut behind him.

13

3 Abstinence Makes the Heart Grow Fonder

"Speaking of secrets," I said to Hector, as I was dusting the bookshelves at closing time, "why exactly is it that you want to keep Hermione Minty's identity secret? It's not a crime to have a pseudonym. It's hardly fraud."

"I have my reasons." Hector kept his eyes on his computer screen. In the absence of any customers, he was proofreading the final manuscript of Hermione Minty's next novel.

With that avenue of conversation proving a cul-de-sac, I changed to a subject that had been bothering me while I was away.

"You know, Hector, I've been thinking. We ought to help Billy cut down on his drinking."

Hector looked up at me, puzzled. "Why? His drinking habits aren't our responsibility."

I washed the cream jug and turned it upside down on the draining board to dry.

"They are a bit," I said. "We're enabling him. We're leading him astray. By serving him your special cream with his tea, we're actively encouraging him to drink more

15

alcohol than he would without us." Hector's 'cream' was a heady milky hooch. "It can't be good for him to start on the booze so early in the day when he comes into the shop for his elevenses."

Hector shrugged. "Old people get up so early in the morning that elevenses to us is like lunchtime to them. Plenty of people enjoy a sherry before lunch. There's even a school of thought that says it's good for them. I bet Joshua Hampton, next door to you, keeps similar hours. He's probably supping his bedtime cocoa by nine o'clock at night."

I glanced down at my new watch, Hector's Christmas present to me, and pursed my lips. That was true, but it didn't let us off the hook.

"It's also illegal to sell alcohol without a licence," I said.

Hector leaned back on his stool and stretched his arms out.

"Ah, but I'm not selling it. I'm not even advertising it. It's just a free gift for certain customers, and it costs me next to nothing to make. If I stopped doing it, those customers might stop coming in. It would make an unwelcome dent in our tearoom takings from Billy for a start. It's all about the bottom line." He set the keyboard to one side and removed the drawer from the till to start cashing up. "You're not the only one who's been doing some thinking over Christmas. Only my thinking involved a calculator, producing evidence that we need to increase our takings. We need more income streams, not less."

"You mean fewer," I said, with the automatic response of a trained English language teacher.

"OK, fewer. All ideas welcome, so don't hold back. You could try getting a few more after-school pupils in for coaching, for a start."

Although I kept the tuition fees for coaching local children in the shop after school, their presence, and their mums', led to significant extra sales in both the bookshop and the tearoom.

"I'll ask Ella whether she can put any more business our way from the village school," I said. "I'm meeting her for a drink after work tomorrow. But why the sudden need? We were doing really well before Christmas. The shop was busy all day, every day, for weeks."

"Yes, but the Christmas shopping season comes only once a year, and next Christmas is a long way off. We've got a quiet time until Valentine's Day at least, or even Easter, when the tourist trade will kick in. And all that time, internet retailers will be quietly winning over customers with deliveries to their doors of orders placed from the comfort of their own homes, often at prices lower than I can offer them. We need to be developing new moneymaking ideas, not abandoning old ones that are working. Besides, I enjoy Billy's company. I'd miss him if he stopped coming in. Not that I'd tell him that."

I tucked the duster in my pocket and picked up the disinfectant spray and dishcloth to clean the tea tables, another of my end-of-day tasks.

"He'd miss us too," I said. "He'd probably still come in anyway. I bet he comes here for the company as much as for the drink. If cheap alcohol was all he was after, he'd drink at home on his own."

Hector walked to the door to turn the 'open' sign to 'closed'.

"I suppose so. But are you sure you're not just letting Tommy frighten you with his talk of detecting secrets?"

17

I laughed. "Frightened of Tommy? Don't be daft. I'm not the one with the secret to hide, Ms Minty." Hector grimaced. "Besides, we don't have to make Billy go cold turkey. How about I start by diluting the cream with ordinary milk? Within a couple of weeks, his tea will be alcohol free, and he'll be none the wiser."

Hector slid a pile of pound coins into a plastic banking bag. "Promise you won't make a citizen's arrest on me in the meantime?"

I thought back to Tommy's advice: *if she loved you, she'd take your side.* I wondered whether Hector was thinking that too. "I promise."

He thumbed through a pile of five-pound notes. "And you won't start watering the brandy in my flat?"

I hesitated. "Actually, I was thinking of going on the wagon myself."

He stopped counting. "Why? Did you have a heavy time of it at Hogmanay? Too much Scotch in Scotland?" His voice was playful, but his eyes were anxious. He looked down quickly at the money in front of him. "Who were you with?"

"Oh, no-one," I said vaguely. "Just my parents." I've never been any good at lying, though it's not for lack of ideas.

Slipping a rubber band round the banknotes, he stuffed them into the safe in the wall behind him and locked the door.

"Well, all the more brandy for me." He flicked off all the light switches except the one for the window display. "But if you change your mind, there'll be a glass waiting for you by the fireside in my flat, and a welcome-home supper, if you fancy it?"

Did he even need to ask, after we'd spent the last two weeks apart?

I slipped into my coat and collected my bags.

"Lock up the shop," I said, "and I'll race you up the stairs."

Much later that evening, when I returned to my cottage with my travelling bags, I noticed the curtains were still open next door. I could see my elderly neighbour Joshua dozing in his usual high-backed armchair, a blanket over his lap, in front of a blazing log fire. He usually closed the curtains at dusk. That he'd left them open suggested that he was either ill or dead or looking out for my return. I hoped it was the latter.

Until that moment, all I had wanted to do was to unpack and dash back up to Hector's, but I had learned since moving into my late aunt's cottage back in the summer that in Wendlebury Barrow everyone looked out for each other. After years of living in anonymous urban flats, I was ready to embrace that philosophy.

I unlocked my front door, set my bags down in the hall and unzipped my handbag to extract my Scottish souvenir for Joshua. Then I closed the door, stepped over the low lavender hedge that divided our front paths, and hammered at his door loud enough to compensate for his hearing impairment. I was relieved to see he immediately stirred from his armchair.

When he opened the door, his enormous smile of welcome made me glad I'd come to see him. He reached out his hands to clasp mine with a surprisingly firm grip. Instinctively, I reached up to kiss him on the cheek, as if greeting my old grandpa. I was so lucky to live next door to him.

As he ushered me through to his front room, I noticed how few Christmas cards stood on his mantlepiece. As a traditionalist, he wouldn't be taking them down until

Twelfth Night the following Friday. I supposed most of his friends and contemporaries must have predeceased him. This would have been his first Christmas without a card – or anything else – from my late Auntie May.

I settled back on his ancient chintz sofa, suddenly feeling very tired. After all, I'd been up since before dawn to catch the earliest flight from Inverness. That seemed like weeks ago now.

"Welcome back, my dear, I am glad to see you," Joshua said, making a slow detour to close the front curtains before settling back into his fireside chair. He clasped his hands contentedly across his chest. "It has been awfully quiet without you next door."

I laughed. "Am I usually so noisy? I'm sorry!"

He shook his head. "I suppose not, but it did feel strangely silent in your absence."

It must have given him a feeling of security to know I was within shouting distance if he had an accident. Although he was still independent, it wouldn't take much to knock him off his feet. The next-door neighbours on the other side were in a huge detached old manor house, their extensive garden muffling any sound between their house and Joshua's.

"I confess I have missed you and your light and cheery presence," he said.

I'd never thought of myself as light and cheery before, but I wasn't about to argue. "I've missed you too," I said automatically, although I realised as I said it that it was true. I leaned across to pass him a small cardboard box patterned in Royal Hunting Stewart tartan. "I brought you back some Edinburgh Rock. A little taste of Scotland that I thought you might enjoy."

He looked doubtful. "Rock? I'm not sure my teeth are up to rock."

I smiled. "Don't worry, it's not solid, like the sticks of rock you buy at the seaside. This is melt-in-the-mouth stuff. You could still enjoy it without any teeth at all."

Although I meant to be encouraging, after I'd spoken I realised I might have sounded rude. But Joshua was unabashed. He set the little box down on the side table beside his armchair.

"Good idea, Sophie, I shall enjoy it at bedtime. That's one of the many joys of growing old: being able to eat as many sweets as you like in bed without brushing your teeth, which just sit in the glass on the bedside cabinet and smile at you."

I admired Joshua's positive attitude.

"So what's new with you?" I asked, trying not to look at his mouth. "Did you have a good Christmas?"

Joshua had been invited to his cousin's in our nearest town, Slate Green, for Christmas Day. I was sorry he had no children or grandchildren to spend it with.

"Very pleasant indeed, thank you. More turkey than I could shake my walking stick at. And you?"

"Lovely, thanks. Mum and Dad were glad to see me, as I hadn't been there since before I moved to Wendlebury in June. A visit home was a bit overdue. But I'm glad to be back. This is my home now really."

"I'm pleased to hear it. Is all well at Hector's House today? And with Hector?"

Joshua didn't miss much. He must have realised that Hector would collect me from the airport and take me straight into work at his bookshop. I hoped Joshua didn't guess what else I'd just been doing with Hector.

"Yes, thanks." I changed the subject before he could probe any further. "Tommy Crowe was in the shop today, at a loose end as school doesn't start until tomorrow. You'll never guess what he had for Christmas."

21

Joshua shook his head. "Probably some new invention that I won't understand, one of those Former Boxes or whatever they call them."

I smiled. "No, not an Xbox. I don't suppose his mum could afford one of those even if she wanted to. Something much more traditional: a detective kit. Sina gave him a book about how to be a detective, and his mum gave him a magnifying glass, a fingerprint kit, and goodness knows what else. All he's missing is the deerstalker cap and pipe."

"Has he detected anything yet?" Joshua's eyes twinkled, knowing how mischievous Tommy Crowe could be.

"Not that I know of, but he's determined to track down unsolved crimes in the village. He seems to think there are plenty to choose from. I hope he's not going to be disappointed. I should think all he'll find will be parking offences and littering, rather than anything more serious."

"Or smuggling," said Joshua, to my surprise. "Or forgery. Or drug abuse. I could name a few guilty parties there for starters. Not that I'm going to give Tommy any tip-offs."

I must have looked startled, because Joshua was quick to comfort me.

"Nothing to worry about, my dear. To each his own. Everyone's welcome to their own devices in our little village."

"Surely you're not condoning crime?"

Joshua sat back in his chair and gazed up at the bright ceiling light, the bulb dazzling beneath its old-fashioned fringed silk shade. I suppose your eyesight needs extra help as you get older.

"Not condoning, my dear, just acknowledging that some activities conducted locally go beyond the letter of the law yet remain unpunished. Distilling spirits, for example."

He returned his rheumy gaze to me, as if checking my reaction.

"Yes, but it's not as if Hector's selling it, or evading tax on it. He gives it away, just as he would home-made cakes, if he ever made any."

Only after I'd spoken did it occur to me that Joshua might not have been referring to Hector.

"Taxation isn't the only reason you need a licence. There are also matters of health. Wood alcohol can damage your eyesight."

Watching Joshua staring unblinkingly beneath the glare of the ceiling light, I wondered whether this was the voice of experience. I swallowed.

Joshua leaned back. "Of course, it was different in the days when we had a village bobby on the beat. You couldn't get away with much then. I remember when young Billy" – he meant old Billy, but, to be fair, Joshua was older than him – "found a beautiful wooden catapult in his Christmas stocking. Our bobby caught him shooting pebbles at the vicar's cat on the village green. So he snatched the catapult straight out of his hand and snapped it in half across his knee. That taught Billy not to do it again." He smiled wryly at the memory. "Of course, we've got a policeman living in the village now, but that's not the same thing as being on the beat. I hear he spends most of his off-duty time indoors with his eyes fixed on his television."

He closed his eyes, not speaking for so long that I wondered whether he'd nodded off. I glanced at the clock and saw it was nearly nine.

23

Suddenly his eyes snapped open.

"But don't let thoughts of local crime worry you, Sophie. I'm sure you'll sleep safe in your bed tonight. Especially with Tommy Crowe on the look-out." That twinkle again. Had he guessed that I'd promised to spend the night with Hector after I'd unpacked? I was glad he'd now drawn his curtains so that he wouldn't see me sneak back up the High Street. Joshua may be old, but he could teach Tommy Crowe a thing or two about detection.

4 Wagons Roll

"Not you too," said Donald, exchanging weary glances with Ella across the bar. All I'd done was ask for a mineral water.

Since returning to Wendlebury, the only alcohol I'd drunk had been a couple of glasses of brandy at Hector's and a drop of Joshua's sloe gin "for warmth", as he put it. But I had resolved to stay dry when I caught up with Ella at The Bluebird.

"At least I didn't say tap water," I said, frowning. "I'm not being mean, I'm just not drinking alcohol."

After the chaos of the first day of term at the village school, Ella had other ideas.

"Well, I'm having a glass of wine, Donald, whatever Sophie's drinking," she said. She turned to me, all wide-eyed innocence. "Why don't you have a white wine spritzer, Sophie? A little drop of wine in a long glass topped up with soda water doesn't really count as an alcoholic drink."

Donald nodded encouragement.

I frowned. "I thought the bubbles got you drunk faster?"

Ella waved a hand dismissively. "No, no, you're thinking of champagne. I'm not suggesting you drink champagne. Not on a January budget."

I gave a tiny nod of assent. "Just a small one, then."

"I wish a few people would stump up for champagne," Donald said, tonging a few ice cubes from an insulated plastic bucket into a long glass. "My takings always slump in January, what with everyone being spent out after Christmas, and not wanting to repeat their New Year hangover."

He picked up a wine glass, filled it to the lower line with chilled Sauvignon Blanc, and tipped the wine into the tumbler.

"Besides, you're doing me a favour," said Ella. "If you don't have at least a tiny drink, you'll be turning me into a solitary drinker. And that is bad."

I held the tumbler steady as Donald topped up the wine with soda water.

"OK, but just the one."

With the pub otherwise empty, Ella and I sat up at the bar to keep Donald company. We perched on the high oak stools with red velvet tops that always make me feel like a candidate on *Blind Date*.

"So tell me, Ella," I asked carefully, "how clever is Tommy Crowe? You must know, having had him at your school for seven years. You must have seen his test results, and that sort of thing."

She considered for a moment. "I wasn't there for his whole seven years. It's three years since he left, and I've been at the school for five, so I can only tell you about his last two years. He's a bright boy, but lacks application in the classroom. His other interests distracted him, and his behaviour held him back. With twenty-nine other children in the class, the teachers sometimes

26

misinterpreted his curiosity as insolence and reacted accordingly."

"I can see why teachers might feel that way."

"But why do you want to know? Has he applied for a Saturday job in the bookshop? He could probably do with a bit of pocket money. His mum's always skint. I don't think she gets anything from his dad."

"He did hint at a Saturday job a while ago, before telling us that he thought all books looked the same. Fortunately he's on to something quite different now. He's setting himself up as a detective. I'm wondering how good his powers of deduction might be."

Polishing glasses behind the bar for want of something better to do, Donald chuckled. "Why, have you got something to hide, Sophie? Are you worried you might get found out?"

"Yes, Sophie, what have you been up to, you bad girl?"

"My conscience is clear, thank you very much. It's others that I'm worried about."

Donald held a port glass up to the light to check for smears. "So there's a gang of you now, is there?" He winked at Ella. "Well, you know what they say. Who was it who once sent a note to his colleagues saying 'Fly at once, all is known', and they all disappeared, never to be seen again?"

"Ooh yes," said Ella. "I bet there's a few people in the village who Tommy could make disappear. He could double up as a conjuror."

I laughed. "It's hard to imagine how he could detect things without getting into trouble. You know, sneaking around places where he shouldn't be, disturbing things better left undisturbed."

Ella leaned forward, clasping her hands with impish glee.

"Sophie, are you sure there's not something you'd like to tell us? You're among friends. You can tell me and Donald, and it will go no further."

"That's right," said Donald, elbows on the counter, poised to receive confidences. "You can spill your heart out here, Sophie, and apart from me and Ella, nobody will be any the wiser. It's not as if there are any other customers about to hear you, more's the pity."

I glanced towards the toilets that stood sentry beside the door that led to the rear courtyard.

"Not even in the loo," he added.

I hesitated. "Actually, Donald, it seems to me as if you're the one who needs assistance, not me. It doesn't seem right that the pub should be so empty at this time of the evening. It's way past tea-time. Is there anything we can do to help?"

Donald arranged the polished glasses on the shelf above the bar. "Well, you could have another round for a start."

Ella shook her head. "Sorry, I've got to drive home soon." I put my hand over the top of my glass in fellow feeling.

Donald set down his tea towel, raised the flap on the bar, and came round to sit beside us on a high stool.

"Sophie, Hector tells me you're a dab hand at this marketing lark. Have you got any ideas that would help me fill the bar in the long, dark winter nights?"

I sipped my drink slowly to give myself time to think, then set the tumbler down on the bar.

"I would have thought that was obvious, Donald. I mean, what falls in the middle of February? The one date that no-one can forget that month?"

"My dog's birthday," said Donald, "but I wouldn't have thought that was much of a draw."

Ella rolled her eyes. "Oh, Donald, you're such a *man*!"

Donald brightened. "Thank you, that's the nicest thing anyone's said to me all day."

"I mean Valentine's Day," I said. "Don't tell me you never bother with Valentine's Day? And you a married man, too."

"Don't worry, I was only kidding, girls," he said, though I suspected he wasn't. "But who wants to spend Valentine's Day in a pub? You ask any bloke what his girlfriend would say if he offered to take her to the pub for Valentine's Day. He'd get short shrift. My wife would kill me if I tried to pull that on her, even if I wasn't a publican myself. If I wanted to do something themed for Valentine's Day, I'd be better off holding a movie night in the meeting room. How about *The Valentine's Day Massacre*? That would go down well with the darts and dominoes teams."

Ella looked reproachful. "There's a world of difference between saying 'Come down the pub for a pint, love' and 'Darling, I've booked us a special table for two at a romantic Valentine's Night dinner with fancy food, sparkling wine, and a chocolatey pudding'."

"And flowers," I added. "Flowers on the table that they can take home."

"And what about a special present for each lovely lady?" said Ella.

"Now who's being sexist?" asked Donald.

Ella shook her head dismissively. "Yes, but sometimes you really want to be treated as a woman," she said.

"You speak for yourself," said Donald.

I flipped a cardboard beer mat over to its blank side and pulled a pen out of my pocket.

"Donald, we're going to make you a plan. You're going to put on a Valentine's Day supper like Wendlebury

Barrow has never seen. And it will more than make up for your quiet January. You wait and see."

I began to write a list of all the things that we'd been suggesting.

"You could give a prize," said Ella brightly. "People always like prizes. How about a hamper?"

Donald scratched his head. "If I've got to supply a hamper, surely I'll have to charge more for the dinner to cover the extra cost? That'll make it more expensive, then nobody will want to come. There's no point running an event at a loss."

Ella wasn't School Business Manager for nothing. "Then get people to sponsor the hamper's contents. Surely there are enough businesses in the village that would stump up local products in return for a bit of PR? If it doesn't cost you a penny to provide the prizes, every raffle ticket sold will be pure profit."

"Each ticket could also count as a discount voucher for their next meal at The Bluebird," I said. "That way everybody is a winner, nobody goes home disappointed, assuming their date doesn't go horribly wrong, and you get repeat business after the special night is over."

Ella nodded in support. "As soon as you've got the hamper together, you can display it to promote your special Valentine's Dinner and start selling raffle tickets too. I bet you'd sell loads in advance."

Donald sat up straighter on his barstool. "The pub will be looking smarter by Valentine's Day, because I've scheduled some interior maintenance work in the next few weeks. A coat of paint all through, some new lighting, that sort of thing. Then in spring I'm going to start on the outside, and turn the back yard into a courtyard garden ready for the summer, with tables and chairs and umbrellas and planters."

Ella raised her eyebrows. "What about that smelly old well in the middle of it?"

I realised I'd never been out the back before, the courtyard currently being the preserve of smokers between drinks. "You've got an old well?"

"Not for much longer. I'm getting it filled in. I had wondered whether I could resurrect it for its original use, and bottle my own water and sell it, but I had the water tested before Christmas, and it's beyond redemption. Too much rubbish has been thrown down there for far too long. Mostly cigarette butts lately, but God knows what else has been ditched down there over the years."

"Can't you just leave it there as an ornament? It seems a shame to seal up something so historic."

"I agree. But I've got a living to make, which won't be helped if some tom fool visitor to my new beer garden decides to taste its waters and dies of nicotine poisoning. Besides, it'll be a family area. I have to think of the children's safety."

"We don't want any of them falling down it, like the pussy cat in the nursery rhyme," Ella laughed.

"Well, if anyone's going to fall in, my money would be on Tommy," I said. "He's been crashing about the shop lately like a golf ball in a pin ball table."

"I wouldn't put it past Tommy to climb down the well out of curiosity," said Ella. "You know, someone once found him inside a wheelie bin?"

I shuddered. "Ugh! I heard about that."

"Anyway, back to Valentine's Night. Would you girls like to help me round up some raffle prizes? You'll be a lot more persuasive than me. There's a drink in it for you if you do."

"I bet Carol would donate a box of chocolates," said Ella.

31

"I can get Hector to give you a romantic novel," I said.

"Ooh, yes," said Ella. "How about one of those signed copies of Hermione Minty's that you had in the shop before Christmas? Got any left?"

"I'm sure there's at least one," I said. "I'll pop it over to you in the morning, Donald."

"Now here's an idea," said Ella. "Why not make it a Minty-themed evening? With a minty menu – Mint Juleps on arrival, lamb cooked with mint, peppermint ice-cream with hot chocolate sauce." She licked her lips in anticipation. "Donald, you can ask the brewery to put in a bottle of Crème de Menthe."

"And a tube of toothpaste," I said. "Joke."

"Thanks, girls," said Donald. "I think that calls for a top up, on the house."

Before I could protest, he'd nipped round the other side of the bar and refilled both our glasses – soda water for Ella, as she was driving, and white wine for me. Well, it would have been rude to refuse.

"So why are you on the wagon?" asked Ella. We'd moved across to a private booth by now, as more people had come into the pub. "Overdid it at Christmas, did you? I've heard what those Scots are like at New Year. They get an extra day off to recover, don't they?"

I nodded. "Yes, two public holidays after New Year's Eve. Or rather, Hogmanay. It's a whole different country up there, you know." I decided to take her into my confidence. "The thing is, Ella, it's a long time since I've been home to my parents' house, and I'd forgotten how much my dad drinks. It's put me right off."

"But I thought he was a university professor?"

I smiled weakly. "And that makes him immune? I don't think so."

32

She pushed her glass away. "I'm sorry, Sophie. I wouldn't have pressed you to have a drink, had I known."

We fell silent. I felt awkward for crushing the jovial atmosphere we'd conjured up with Donald. Ella tried to strike a brighter note.

"I wonder what Hermione Minty gets her other half for Valentine's Day?" she said. "It must be hard to keep some surprises up your sleeve when you're pumping all your romantic ideas into the pages of your books every day."

I was looking forward to finding out.

5 Distinctly Minty

"Donald's Valentine's dinner sounds wonderful to me, Sophie," said Carol, pulling her apron over her head and tying it behind her back. Having her long-lost daughter Becky and grandson Arthur move in with her just before Christmas had slowed down her morning routine. "I wish I had someone to go with."

"You never know. Valentine's Day is still over a month away."

Carol put her hands in her apron pockets. "You're right, I should look on the bright side. New year, new beginnings. I'll be happy to provide something for the hamper. A box of chocolates, you say?"

"Peppermint creams, if you've got them." I spotted a familiar dark green box on the sweet counter. "Donald's giving the whole evening a minty theme – Hermione Minty, that is."

Carol looked wistful. "That sounds wonderful. Becky gave me a signed copy of her latest novel for Christmas. Wasn't that kind? Although the arrival of Becky and Arthur was the best Christmas present ever, I can't get enough of Hermione Minty's books, can you?"

"I've never actually read any." As I said it, I realised I'd missed a trick. Although romantic novels weren't my thing, reading Minty's books would help me get to know Hector better. After all, don't writers put their hearts and souls into their books?

Carol raised her hands. "Oh, Sophie, you don't know what you're missing. You're in for a real treat. Funny thing is, although everyone round here has read her, she doesn't seem famous further afield. Becky said she'd never even heard of Hermione Minty before she came to live with me. I can't understand it."

"I expect she sells most of her books online," I said quickly. "As ebooks, you know."

Carol shook her head. "I can't be doing with ebooks. Give me a proper book any day. One you can read in the bath without electrolysing yourself."

I suppressed a smile. "I don't think ebooks ever electrocuted anyone. It's not like using a toaster in the bath."

Carol wrinkled her nose. "I wouldn't want to do that either. The steam would make the toast go soggy. Anyway, if you want to take a box of mints over to Donald, help yourself. I must get on now. I'm a bit behind this morning. I spent far too long giving little Arthur his breakfast."

She didn't look in much of a muddle to me, but Carol's standards for orderliness were rather higher than mine.

I picked up the chocolates, and tucked one of the shop's business cards from the counter under the ribbon around the box to give Carol credit for the donation. She would be having as much trouble with her profits as Donald during these lean post-Christmas weeks, especially as she had just taken on two extra mouths to feed. Her daughter Becky, as an unemployed single mother, would not be contributing much to the household financially.

"Which is the best book of Minty's to start with?" I asked, guessing that Carol, as a diehard romantic, would be familiar with her complete works.

"Oh, the very first one, *Angel Heart*."

"I'll start on it tonight," I said, hoping to enjoy it as much as Carol had. "And thanks for the mints. I'll get Donald to give you a free raffle ticket as a thank you."

"Or find me a nice man to go to the Valentine's Dinner with," she said quietly. "All I want is one man for one night. Is that too much to hope for?"

I smiled sympathetically. "You never know, perhaps you'll get one for your birthday tomorrow."

I meant it as a joke, but she took me at my word.

"Yes, never say die!" she said brightly, and patted her hair into place.

"I would have thought the answer was obvious."

Hector, busy removing Christmas decorations from the shop window, climbed down from the stepladder.

"Well, it might be, if only I knew what the question was."

He brushed his hands on his trousers to get the dust off them and crossed the room to sit down at a tearoom table. Taking the hint, I went to switch the kettle on.

"The question of how to boost your profits. It's easy. You just need to put more effort into promoting your Minty books."

Hector pointed to the central display table, where there was always at least one prominent pile of them. "Exhibit A," he said. "There are some in the window too."

I wasn't going to let him off that lightly.

"Becky had never heard of Hermione Minty before she came to Wendlebury. And she's quite well read." I didn't want to overpraise Becky. Swapping literary jokes was meant to be a game that Hector played with me, and I wasn't keen that she'd started joining in. "Why ever not, when she's so popular here?"

Hector looked guarded. "It's not that easy, Sophie. I'd rather do something else to boost my income. Start a proper series of author talks, for example, with other authors. That'd be a good idea."

I shook my head. "You're selling yourself short, Hector. I don't believe you've tried to get your books into other shops, have you?"

His sullen silence served as a confession. Was it simply modesty holding him back? I tried a different tack.

"You and I know how well the books do here. They're a major contributor to the shop's profits. If they're that good, it's selfish not to offer other booksellers the opportunity to increase their takings."

Hector frowned. "I only make such a big profit on them because I publish them myself and get them at cost price. Other booksellers would need a cut of the cover price, which would not leave much for me. The game wouldn't be worth the candle."

I took two cookies from a jar on the counter and passed one to him.

"Perhaps if you told them that Hermione Minty is a fellow bookseller, they'd stock your books on more generous terms."

"But I can't do that without revealing my real identity."

I shrugged. "Does that really matter? Perhaps you should give the game away. It would make a great news story in *The Bookseller*. You'd get orders from bookshops all over the country. It's not as if members of the public read *The Bookseller*. Your secret would be safe in Wendlebury."

"No, but other journalists read it. The national newspapers are always running stories about bookshops and booksellers – the death of the ebook, the death of print, the closure of bookshops – nearly always getting it wildly wrong. So there's every reason to think my name would end up in the nationals. No thank you, Sophie, I'm happy as I am – quiet and private, with mid-range but respectable sales."

"But surely if it did get out, you'd attract more customers. People would flock to the bookshop, and from further afield. You'd not only sell more Minty books, but more stock in general."

I put a pot of tea in front of him, sat down and leaned forward.

"Hector," I began, "what's the real reason you don't want people to find out you're Hermione Minty?"

He sat up straight on his chair, looking as guilty as if I'd caught him with his fingers in the till. Not that it would have mattered, as the till was his.

I narrowed my eyes, wishing I had Tommy's magnifying glass to use as a jokey prop.

"Aha, you are undone!"

He glanced down at his flies.

"No, not that sort of undone. I mean, I've caught you out. There's something you're not telling me. If it's just a case of needing to take your books to other shops, I'm here to cover for your time spent away from Hector's House. Or I could take them for you. I could be your rep. But I think there's something else stopping you. I wish you'd tell me what it is."

Hector pursed his lips, stood up, and marched across to the other side of the shop, where he pretended to tidy an already pristine bookshelf. Then after a few minutes of frosty silence, he swung round to address me as if he'd been building up to it.

"All right, then, have it your way."

I opened my mouth to congratulate him on making the right decision, but he put up his hand to stop me.

"Before you ask, I'm not going to start touting my wares to other bookshops, or reveal all to *The Bookseller*. But I do think we might use social media to raise awareness and boost sales of my ebooks. After all, I use them to spread the word about events in the shop, and I know the shop's got a good following. You'd need to set up accounts for Minty, of course, so it looks like she's tweeting and Facebooking herself, but it's not impossible."

"Not impossible? It would be easy-peasy, Hector. Of course, ideally she should be using social media to chat with her fans, not just telling them to buy her books."

He looked so horrified that I backtracked.

"On the other hand, you could automate it, setting up some posts on one of those scheduling services that tweets every so often for you. I'll do it for you, if you like."

"How about a compromise?" He had his serious face on. "I'll allow you to give Hermione a bit of a shout-out on social media, provided you keep my identity and the shop's completely secret. In any case, I'm all tweeted out keeping the Hector's House account up to date. I can't be doing with another one to monitor. I'm happy to delegate that to you. And to keep my distance from it."

I smiled encouragingly. I knew instinctively this was a positive step forward for Hermione Minty, for the shop's financial well-being, and for us. This kind of teamwork, sharing success together, could only bring us closer.

I went over to give him a grateful hug, despite his no-hugs-on-duty rule.

"I'll start the accounts up as soon as I get a moment at the weekend. Trust me. I know what I'm doing."

The shortest day was long past, but it was still getting dark so early that when I strolled home past the pub after work, it felt like night-time. The yellow glow from the village shop cut through the misty evening air like a lighthouse beacon. Although I didn't need anything from the shop, I found myself pushing open its front door, drawn towards its promise of warmth and light.

The jangle of the bell made Becky and Tommy break off their conversation at the counter and look round to see me.

"Hi, Sophie," said Becky, a slight edge in her voice. I wondered whether Tommy had said something to upset her. Not knowing much about her background, he could easily have said something awkward or embarrassing without meaning to. My instinct was to protect them both from each other.

Tommy's school backpack dangled from one shoulder, reminding me of a health-and-safety diagram about the causes of bad backs.

"Haven't you been home since you got off the school bus, Tommy? Your mum will be wondering where you are."

He glanced up at the clock behind the counter. "Is it tea-time already? No wonder I'm hungry." He gave Becky an apologetic wave. "Sorry, Becky, I'd better run."

I held the door open for him to leave, closed it gently behind him, then returned to the counter, picking up a copy of the local paper as an excuse for visiting.

"Are you OK, Becky?"

Becky frowned. "Yes, thanks, Sophie. But Tommy was asking some awkward questions about Mum that I didn't want to answer."

I was touched that she was already calling Carol 'Mum', though they still barely knew each other. I hoped that if I kept quiet, she'd elaborate about Tommy's line of questioning.

"You see, he saw this Christmas card from Mum's secret admirer and assumed it was from my dad. We should have taken it down with the Christmas decorations, but Mum couldn't bring herself to put it in the recycling."

She took a large glittery card down from the shelf behind the counter and passed it to me. On the front, a jovial snowman and snowwoman were holding hands and smiling sweetly enough to make me smile back at them. I opened the card to read the inside.

Happy Christmas, Carol. Ted. Xxx

"Who's Ted?" I asked.

"I don't know. I think Mum knows, but she won't tell me. She just said, 'Oh, no-one'. He must be someone, obviously, but he's definitely not my dad. My dad's name is Albert. At least, that's what it says on my birth certificate, and I've got no reason to believe it's not true, even though Mum gave me her own surname."

I paused. "Whoever he is, it sounds as if his love is unrequited."

I wondered why Carol hadn't alluded to him when we'd been talking that morning about dates for Donald's Valentine's dinner.

"Now I'm worried that Tommy will tell everyone my dad's called Ted," said Becky. "Not helpful." She paused.

"I don't suppose your real dad would be pleased to have someone else credited with being your father," I said. I hoped that remark wouldn't make Becky clam up.

"Who cares what he thinks?" said Becky. "He never considered my feelings, or my mum's. I've never even met him."

I was glad when she steered the conversation back to the mysterious Ted.

"Mum says there's no-one called Ted in the village, and she doesn't really have a social life beyond Wendlebury," said Becky. "Most of the things she does here are for women only, like the knitting circle and WI. The only romance she gets is in novels, women's magazines, or on the telly."

I turned the card over to see if there were any clues to its origin. Ted had removed the price label, but it bore the own-brand logo of a supermarket down in Slate Green.

"Perhaps it's someone who came into the shop and took a shine to her?" Then I remembered the baker who had been enquiring about her after the nativity play. He'd been supplying the village shop with his almost inedible cakes on a trial basis since before Christmas. It came back to me now. I thought his name was Ted.

I glanced along the aisle to an untouched tray of sturdy doughnuts, their watery icing seeping into the sponge. Wandering casually across, I picked one up with the metal tongs and dropped it into a paper bag.

"I wouldn't if I were you," said Becky, taking the bag from me and folding over the top. From the weight of the bag, I suspected I'd end up putting the doughnut out for the birds, after a good soak so as not to break their little beaks. At least if someone bought his cakes, it might give Ted a bit longer to win Carol over.

"When's your next cake delivery due?" I asked casually.

"Tomorrow, I think," said Becky, flicking open the order book. "Mum's birthday, by the way. I'm going to do the afternoon shift so she can go to the hairdresser's as a birthday treat. It's about time she had some treats after all she does for everyone else."

I was glad Becky didn't see Carol solely as a free source of board and lodging.

"I'll pop in with a card and a present for her tomorrow," I said. There'd no doubt be something suitable at Hector's House.

"Enjoy your doughnut," she called after me, with a mischievous smile. "Don't forget we stock indigestion remedies too."

6 Tracking Ted

"Does the name Ted mean anything to you, Hector?" I asked as I cleared away the debris from Billy's elevenses the next day.

"In what context? Ted Hughes, Poet Laureate? Ted Allbeury, MI6 thriller writer? TED Talks, the online education distributor? Ted Baker, fashion designer?"

"Ted *the* Baker rather than Ted Baker. Wasn't that baker we met before Christmas called Ted? You know, the one who donated those delicious filled pitta breads for the buffet after the nativity play."

"And the leaden mince pies."

"Tommy liked them. He said they were very filling."

"Like ballast in a hot air balloon, perhaps."

Hector pulled open the old oak filing card index on his desk. His antique-dealer parents had salvaged it from Slate Green public library when it went digital, and it was one of the few items of theirs that Hector retained when he turned their antique shop into his bookshop. I loved the gleaming oak, smelling of furniture polish, that matched the shelves lining the shop.

He pulled out a business card from the B section.

"You're right, Sophie, he was a Ted. Ted's Treats, 12 The Rise, Slate Green. That's an auspicious address for a baker."

He passed me a small card the colour and texture of wholemeal flour, and I took it gratefully.

"Hurrah!"

"And being called Ted is cause for celebration because...? You like teddy bears?"

"More than I like his cakes." My stomach still felt sore from last night's doughnut. "But I liked him, and even better, he likes Carol. Did you know he sent her a big Christmas card with kisses? He must be keen."

Hector smiled indulgently. "Good for Carol."

"She's pretending to Becky that she doesn't know who it's from. When Tommy saw it, he asked Becky if Ted was her father."

Hector rolled his eyes.

"Do you think Becky's father will ever come back to the village? I'd hate for him to come barging back in and spoil things for her and Carol now."

"He wouldn't dare. There'd be a queue of people to thump him if he did, besides Carol and Becky."

"You can include me too. I'm so angry on her behalf for what he did to her."

"Billy would be at the front of the line. Bertie may have been his esteemed elder brother when he was little, but Billy never forgave him for what he did to Carol."

"But there must be twenty years between Billy and Carol."

Hector nodded. "Even more with Bertie. But in those days, there weren't many single women of their own age in the village, as most of them had married or moved away, or both. My mum reckoned Billy rather fancied Carol himself. My mum would make a special trip to

46

punch Bertie on the nose if she knew he was coming back."

"Goodness, is she that fierce?"

Hector smiled. "She is when her maternal instinct is aroused. Remember, she was Carol's mum's best friend, and when she saw what the whole situation did to her friend – and indeed to Carol – she was incensed. As was your Auntie May."

I still remembered visiting Carol's stroke-ridden mother with Auntie May, when I used to come and stay in Wendlebury in the school holidays.

"Speaking of parents," he said quickly, "I wanted to talk to you about coming to meet mine. Shall we fix up a date soon?"

That cast all thoughts of Ted and Carol from my mind.

"Wow. Ok. Yes, thanks."

I got out my diary, realised it was last year's, and chose a new one from the stationery rack.

"I'll confirm it when I go down to see them this weekend," he said, ringing my purchase up on the till.

Then I chose a birthday card and a book of baby knitting patterns for Carol's birthday, wrapped the present up, and determined to take them to her before she departed to the hairdresser's.

"I found it here on the counter when I came out of the toilet," said Tommy, looking hungrily at the cake in front of him. He went to dip his finger in the lavish pink icing for a taste, but I slapped his hand away.

"But you said Becky left you in charge while she took the baby home to get him some dry trousers. What were you doing in the toilet?"

When he started to tell me in graphic detail, I interrupted.

"I didn't want a description. I meant, why did you abandon your post?"

"I had to go to the toilet, of course." Tommy looked at me as if I was an idiot.

"Yes, but anyone could have come in and raided the till while you left the shop unattended."

"Come to think of it, I did see a white van drive off as I came back out."

"There you are, then."

"But I think it was only that baker guy. You know, the one with the van without any markings."

I groaned. I must have just missed Ted.

"But I wanted to speak to him. He's the man who sent Carol that Christmas card."

"He's sent her a birthday card too now."

Tommy held up a ripped envelope.

"You've opened her birthday card?"

"I thought it might be an important message. Or a clue. Which it is. Look—" He held up a card showing a glittering illustration on the front of a giant bouquet of roses. "It says his name. Ted. Ted Love."

I took it from him and opened it to read the inscription.

"Love, Ted. Love comma Ted. He means love from Ted. Love's not his surname."

Tommy grabbed the card back.

"But look at his writing. He's a madman. My detective book says that only mad people write everything in capitals."

"Or people who want to make sure that the recipient can read their message. It looks perfectly normal to me, Tommy."

"Maybe he doesn't want to reveal his true identity by signing his usual signature. Maybe he's got a soo – a poo – a fake name, like an author."

"A pseudonym."

"Yes, one of them. Like in a ransom note. Perhaps he's secretly Henry Minty."

"You mean Hermione?"

"Is that how you say it? I thought it was a funny way to spell Henry."

"But whatever makes you think Ted is Hermione Minty in disguise?"

"Well, somebody has to be. My mum says no-one knows who Minty is, but that he lives in a village in the countryside. It says so on his books. So I've told her I'm going to track down this Minty person because Mum wants to meet him. She loved that book you made me buy her for Christmas. I've never seen her sit and read a book before, but now she's mad about books. Well, Hermione Minty's books, anyway."

I should have felt more pleased. "But Wendlebury Barrow is just one village out of hundreds in the country."

"Yes, but it's got to be one of the most important villages, hasn't it? I think it would be a very good place for a writer person to live. I mean, your auntie was a writer, and she lived here, didn't she?"

I looked at him for a moment, trying to gauge whether he was joking, but quickly realised he was deadly serious. To Tommy, born and raised in the village, with very little opportunity to travel beyond it other than on the school bus, Wendlebury probably felt like the centre of the world. He wasn't like me, or indeed my Auntie May, a seasoned traveller who had lived and worked abroad, while keeping her cottage here as a bolthole.

49

Not everyone in the village had such broad horizons. Some of the elderly had lived here all their working lives, never going far enough away to need passports, and the very young hadn't yet escaped the gravitational pull of the village. But soon enough, they'd leave for university or vocational training or college or jobs elsewhere. Only a few of them returned, and only when they were earning enough to get on the housing ladder, which for many meant never.

I realised I was exceptionally lucky to have inherited May's cottage. My rental days were over. Whether Wendlebury Barrow would eventually become the centre of my universe remained to be seen. But while Hector was around, for now I was happy to be the moon to his Earth – and think of the effect the moon has on the Earth's tides.

Tommy coughed theatrically, dragging me back to our conversation.

"Tommy, you do know, don't you, that Hermione is a girl's name? You know, like Hermione Granger in the Harry Potter books." I crossed my fingers behind my back. "Surely you don't think those romantic novels were written by a man?"

Tommy was undaunted. "You're being very sexist, miss. He might be a soppy man." He pulled out his trusty diary from his Parka pocket. "I'm making a note of that. Pretending to be a baker could be a cunning disguise to put us off the scent. That's why his cakes are so bad. He's not really a baker at all. And that's why he hasn't got anything written on his van."

I groaned. "Listen, let's forget about Ted for the moment. Before Becky gets back, you need to check the till to make sure no-one filched all the money while you were in the toilet. You don't want to get her into trouble.

And while you're doing that, I'll buy another envelope so we can seal the card again so it isn't obvious you've already opened it. You don't want to spoil Carol's birthday, do you?"

Tommy had the decency to look contrite.

Just as I'd sealed the envelope and carefully written Carol's name on it in anonymous capitals, who should pull up outside but Ted? Tommy and I lapsed into a guilty silence as Ted got out of his van and walked into the shop.

"Hello," he said, sounding a little awkward as he stood on the threshold, with both of us staring at him. "I just realised I'd forgotten to take the stale cakes away."

He strolled slowly down to the C shelf, so slowly that I realised he was playing for time, hoping that Carol might return if he hung about long enough. He probably hadn't forgotten the stale cakes at all. This was simply a pretext to return. He was getting braver.

I followed him down the aisle to talk to him without Tommy joining in. "Ted," I began tentatively. "It is Ted, isn't it? Do you remember we met at the nativity play? My boyfriend, Hector, was tucking into those delicious pitta breads you donated. I wrote the play."

He set the tray of cakes down again and turned to offer his hand for me to shake.

"Yes, of course, you're Sophie, aren't you?"

"Yes, that's right."

His wide brown eyes disarmed me for a moment. Though his handshake was strong and manly, he had the helpless look of a fawn.

"Tommy told me you'd left Carol a birthday cake. That's really kind of you."

"And a card." He looked anxiously to the counter to make sure it was still there. I hoped his eyesight wasn't sharp enough to recognise that it wasn't his handwriting on the envelope now. "I was rather hoping I might catch her here earlier, but she was at the hairdresser's. I expect she'll be back soon." He glanced hopefully at the door.

"If you haven't got any more deliveries to make, I'm sure you'll be welcome to wait," I said gently.

He stood up a little straighter. "You don't think she'd mind?"

I smiled. "I should think she'd be delighted. It's not every day a tall, dark, handsome stranger brings you a home-made birthday cake."

He thought for a moment. "Well, if you say so…"

"I do. It's very kind of you to make her a special birthday cake, and I think you deserve to be thanked in person. And you never know where it might lead…"

I stopped short, realising I might be overstepping the mark.

"But if you'll excuse me, I must get back to Hector's House. I work there with him, and we don't close for another hour. Do call in any time you're passing, if you fancy a cup of tea. We've got a very pleasant tearoom, and we'll always be glad to see you."

He reached out to shake my hand in farewell. I noticed what muscular fingers he had, even though he was quite old, fifty at least. Very good hands for a baker, I thought, brilliant for kneading bread.

Deciding to bring my gift back later to give to Carol in person, I scurried towards the door, but not too soon to hear Tommy calling out, "Here, are you Minty?" followed by Ted's startled reply, "A bit – I did take a breath mint before I came in."

I'd like to have been a fly on the wall to hear the rest of that conversation.

7 Counter Spy

I'd barely had time to regale Hector with the news about the birthday cake when Ted appeared in our doorway.

"Carol turned me down," he said glumly, striding over to join me in the tearoom.

My jaw dropped. I'd have thought Carol would have grabbed with both hands the opportunity for a date with a man like Ted. Or indeed the man himself. He seemed so suitable and keen. If I'd been twice my age, I might even have fancied him myself.

Hector, busy replenishing the historical fiction section, turned around to cast a sympathetic look in Ted's direction. "I'm sorry to hear that, mate," he said gently. "Did she give you a reason?"

"She told me there's someone else."

"Really?" I could hardly believe it. "I can't imagine who."

When Hector shot me a restraining look, I realised my comment might have sounded a bit rude.

Ted sank down into a chair at a tea table. "Do you think she was just saying that to get rid of me?"

I put a clean cup and saucer in front of him and switched on the kettle. I didn't need to ask. The man needed tea.

"No, of course not. Maybe you took her by surprise. Perhaps she was a bit overcome, it being her birthday and everything."

He shook his head sadly. "I don't know, she sounded pretty sure of her answer. She cancelled my cake order too. I don't know, I don't seem to be able to get anything right lately."

I went to join him at the table.

"That boy Tommy who was hanging round down there, is he her son or her nephew or something? He was asking me some odd personal questions. Then he asked me for my autograph." He sighed. "It's probably my own fault. Perhaps I didn't ask in the right way. I was a bit overwhelmed when she arrived back from the hairdresser's, looking lovely. I must have made a hash of it. That's the story of my life."

I smiled sympathetically. "I hope Tommy didn't put you off. Count yourself lucky he didn't ask you for your fingerprints."

"Oh, but he did," said Ted. "But only after he accused me of being Carol's daughter's father." He looked wistful for a moment. "I wish. She's very beautiful, isn't she?"

"Becky? Yes, she is." I got up to fill the teapot and brought it over to the table.

Ted shook his head. "Becky's pretty as a picture, but I was meaning Carol. I've always thought women get more beautiful as they get older, when their experiences have been etched on their faces. I like women with character. And you can see Carol's good nature in her face, with all those smiling lines. You can see in a woman's lines whether she's got it in her to be happy."

54

"That's our Carol all right," said Hector quietly. I suspected he was as touched as I was by Ted's candid tribute. "By the way, don't worry about Tommy. He's harmless enough, just a little boy playing policemen with his Christmas detective kit."

I poured us each a cup of tea, and we added milk in silence, as if it was a bonding ritual – which I suppose it is, really. I was on the brink of offering Ted some of Hector's alcoholic cream to cheer him up, but then remembered he was driving, and I was meant to be on the wagon.

"You leave it with me, Ted," I said, patting his hand. "We've got your phone number. Hector's still got your card from the nativity play. I'll have a quiet word with Carol on your behalf, then I'll call or text you. It's probably nothing but a misunderstanding. She's not always the best person with words."

He smiled wistfully. "Yes, I'd noticed that. It's very endearing."

When Ted had gone, Hector refilled our cups, tipping the pot right up to drain it.

"Are you sure you know what you are doing, Sophie? You don't know Ted from Adam. All we know is that he bakes dreadful cakes and fabulous bread. Is that enough to justify setting him up with a dear but vulnerable friend?"

I wrinkled my nose. "There's something about him that makes me think he's perfect for Carol. There are few enough single men passing through this way. Who knows when Carol will get another opportunity like this for a date? Especially now she's got competition from the beautiful Becky." I pictured Ted's kindly face. "He's got lovely warm eyes. And a very firm handshake."

Hector looked arch. "Warm hands, cold heart?"

I shook my head. "No, he's a teddy bear. But Carol's refusal – now there's a mystery that needs solving." I got up and cleared the table. "Where's Tommy when you really need him? I'm off to make discreet enquiries."

"Carol, what were you thinking, sending that nice baker packing?" On my way home, I called in to see her and deliver her birthday present from me and Hector. Well, from Hector, strictly speaking, as he let me take it off the shelf without paying for it.

Carol avoided eye contact, fiddling with the gift-wrapped parcel.

"You can open it now if you like," I said "It is your birthday."

She grabbed a sharp knife from under the counter and slit the sticky tape to remove the wrapping paper without damaging it. After folding the paper neatly and setting it to one side, she held up the book of knitting patterns to show me, as if I wouldn't have known what the parcel contained.

I smiled approvingly. "Some of those things will look lovely on little Arthur. Now, tell me, why did you turn down Ted's invitation for a date? He seems ever so nice. An utter gent."

She sighed. "I can't lie to you, Sophie. The thing is, there's someone else with a prior claim on me." She leaned forward confidentially, although there was no-one else in the shop now

"What? Only last night you were telling me you wanted to meet a new man for your birthday. What happened? Were you swept off your feet by a stranger at the hairdresser's? Now that's what I call a lightning courtship."

She looked away for a moment, as if wondering how much to tell me.

"Go on," I said, intrigued.

She sighed again and stared at the counter. "Sophie, please don't tell a soul – not Becky nor Billy, nor even Hector."

I crossed my heart with my forefinger.

"It's Becky's father. He phoned me this morning."

"What?" That was the last answer I was expecting. "How did he even know where to find you?"

She pressed her lips together into a thin line. "I've been in the same place all my life. The shop phone number's the same as it's ever been. My home address hasn't changed. I'm not exactly hard to trace. But there's worse. He knows that Becky's here. And Arthur."

"But he hasn't had anything to do with them. He hasn't even met them before, has he?"

She shook her head. "No, he was a clean pair of heels before Becky was even born. And I hadn't heard a word from him since. Then this morning he phoned my home number, and Becky answered. She had no idea who was calling, and when a strange man asked if that was Carol speaking, she said, 'This is her daughter, Becky.' He fell in at once, even though he didn't know what name I'd given her before I... before, well, you know... before she was taken off by the adoption people."

She stopped to blow her nose and wipe her eyes. I felt awful for making her cry on her birthday. When I was a little girl, we used to say if you cried on your birthday, you'd cry every day for the rest of the year.

"Arthur was shouting in the background, and Becky said to Bertie, 'Please excuse my noisy little boy', so of course he put two and four together."

"I hope you put the phone down on him."

She put her hands to her flushed cheeks. "How could I? He's Becky's father. And he's fallen on hard times."

"Self-induced, no doubt. Did he ask you for money?"

For a moment she didn't reply.

"Yes, he asked me for money," she said finally.

I gasped. "How dare he? You didn't offer him any, did you?"

"No. But he's returning to Wendlebury. So I could hardly say yes to Ted with Bertie hanging over my head, could I?"

I tried to put that image out of my mind.

"He's not expecting to come and stay with you, surely?"

"No, at the bed and breakfast at The Bluebird."

I frowned. "I didn't know Donald did b and b."

"He doesn't. I told him The Bluebird's accommodation was closed twenty years ago by the previous landlord, but Bertie wouldn't believe me. He told me he'd come anyway. He said it would be a good idea if we got back together for the sake of the children."

"I hope he's not thinking he can waltz in and start playing happy families after what he did to you?"

Carol shook her head. "I told him that was out of the question. Besides, I've nowhere to put him. Becky and Arthur have got my spare room. I suppose he could stay with his brother Billy. They might still keep in touch, for all I know. Billy's the only close relative he's got left now, and even though they fell out years ago, blood's thicker than beer."

I couldn't believe the man's nerve. "How is it going to help Becky or Arthur to have a reprobate who abandoned you without remorse hanging around them? God knows what bad habits he's acquired while he's been away. He might be a drunk or violent or an abuser—"

Carol's tears were flowing freely now. "He was all that before he left Wendlebury in the first place. But he is still Becky's father, so doesn't he have rights? Doesn't Becky have rights to him? And little Arthur to his granddad?"

"The person whose rights I'm most concerned about is you. Bertie abdicated his rights to any part in your life before Becky was born. You're just starting to build a precious and meaningful relationship with her and the baby, so don't let him spoil things – or sponge off you, either. Besides, you've got enough new financial responsibilities with Becky and Arthur to care for."

Carol sniffed, trying to pull herself together. "You're right. And honestly, I know it's unkind of me, but I've never really forgiven him for what he did to me and my parents. Things could have been so different." She gazed down at the book of knitting patterns, the cover of which showed a picture of four beautiful children, from a baby up to a four-year-old. "Now I stop to think about it, you've made me see him in a different light. And I realise now how angry I am deep inside. Honestly, Sophie, if he turned up on my doorstep, I don't know what I'd do, but it wouldn't be pleasant for him."

I tried not to look as pleased as I felt at her change of heart. "All the more reason not to turn Ted down. Surely you deserve another chance with a decent guy after all these years. Perhaps if you just told Bertie straight out there was someone else, especially a tall, strong man like Ted, he'd stay away."

"Yes, but I couldn't bear to tell Ted all the shameful details of my past. He would go right off me."

I took her hand. "Carol, I know you're a very honest person, but sometimes a little white lie can be for the best. Bertie will have no way of knowing that Ted isn't your long-standing partner. For all he knows, Ted might have swept you off your feet like a knight on a white charger, and be standing by, ready to skewer with his lance anyone who dares to upset you."

Carol brightened. "What a lovely thought."

"Besides, you don't need to tell Ted about Bertie if you don't want to. Or you could tell him an edited version of events. Your version. It's your call."

She covered her eyes with her hands. "Oh, Sophie, what have I done? I'm so mixed up I don't know what I'm doing. I've turned the wrong one down. And I've cancelled Ted's trial cake order. Though to be honest, I should have done that ages ago, because his cakes are terrible. I only kept ordering from him because I liked him. So I'm scuppered. Again. Still—" she sniffed and forced a smile "—at least I've got Becky and Arthur. Although for all I know, they may only be staying because they've got nowhere else to go. It's probably only a matter of time before they leave me too."

I shook my head. "I don't think that. The longer they stay with you, the more they'll come to know and love you. And what better place than Wendlebury to raise a family?"

She wiped her eyes with the back of her hand.

"Even if they don't stay around that long, you'll have had the chance to get to know each other, and I'm sure she'll stay in touch."

"But what if Bertie turns up?" Her voice cracked. "I fear I'll do something drastic. He's hurt me so much, all I want to do is to hurt him back. Which isn't like me at all."

"Well, all the more reason to cut him dead if he phones again," I said. "When someone starts turning you into someone you are not, that's the time you ought to say goodbye to them for good."

8 All A-Twitter

Spending Sunday alone while Hector visited his parents, I was able to concentrate on building Hermione Minty's new Twitter account – the first step in raising her profile beyond Hector's House. I found it easy to set up her account as I'd used social media quite a bit when I was working abroad. It was a good way to share news and photos of my travels in my peripatetic teaching jobs without having to contact friends and relations individually. I'd even made reluctant tweeps out of my parents. My dad didn't follow anyone but me on Twitter, showing my mum every post on his phone. It was just as well we shared a surname, or people would have thought he was a stalker.

I was glad Minty had such an unusual name so that I could nab @HermioneMinty as her Twitter handle. I cobbled together a description for her profile, and found online a royalty-free photo of a woman in a floaty dress, her face screened by lustrous wavy blonde hair. I added an alluring header image with a backdrop of misty honeysuckle. The perfume would have been heavenly.

Next I made a long list of tweets to send, each coupled with the cover of the appropriate book, and a link to where readers could buy it.

I felt very clever.

Then I raided Auntie May's ancient *Oxford Dictionary of Quotations* for quotes about love and romance and added lots of those. People often retweet memorable quotes.

Next I made Minty follow everyone in the Romantic Novelists' Association, in hope that they'd follow her back.

By the end of the evening, Hermione Minty had 237 followers and had tweeted forty-six times.

When I checked the clock, wondering why my eyes felt so tired, it was gone midnight. Proud of my efforts, I made Minty say "Goodnight and sweet romantic dreams" to all her followers, before retiring to bed for some sweet romantic dreams of my own. These were slightly marred by Hector being attired throughout in a long floral dress and a white linen bonnet.

"Hermione Minty's been retweeted by Katie Fforde," I said proudly next morning, showing Hector the evidence on my phone. "It doesn't get much better than that."

I clicked across to Katie Fforde's account to share one of her tweets out of courtesy. Then I checked Minty's overnight followers and followed them back, before realising an obvious omission in the set-up.

"Oh gosh, she's not following Hector's House!" I quickly rectified my error, then retweeted Hector's latest post about our January sale of diaries and calendars.

"I'd better make sure Hector's House follows Hermione," said Hector, gamely. "I wouldn't want her to think me rude."

"You could always ask Hermione Minty to come and give a talk here," said Julia. "She lives in the Cotswolds."

It was the Wendlebury Writers' first meeting of the new year. As we sat in the Hector's House tearoom after closing time, all our thoughts were focused on planning something different and special for the coming season. Well, that and the delicious Victoria sponge that I'd saved for us to share. I'd been telling the others about Hector's plans to start a new series of author events to boost the bookshop's takings.

"How do you know where Hermione Minty lives?" I asked, genuinely puzzled.

"I've just started following her on Twitter," said Julia brightly. "It says on her profile that she lives in the Cotswolds."

She dug in her capacious handbag for her phone, dislodging notebooks, pens, tissues and make-up to find it. Tapping the Twitter icon, she quickly found Minty's account and held it up to show us.

"See? Cotswolds."

I cursed myself for being so stupid. In Minty's official bio on her website and in the "About the Author" section in her books, it said only that she lived in an English village. I'd added Cotswolds as the location to her Twitter profile, thinking it would be a good selling point. After all, the Cotswolds are the perfect setting for romantic novelists. Katie Fforde lives in the Cotswolds, as does M C Beaton and loads of others. It had never occurred to me that anyone I knew might follow Hermione Minty on Twitter. I'd been targeting people I didn't know – all those who would never have the chance to see her books piled high at Hector's House. I didn't expect her to start bonding with my neighbours.

"Then she's got no excuse to refuse if we're on her doorstep," said Dinah, with a finality that alarmed me.

Julia clapped her hands together excitedly. "She might like to launch her next book here at Hector's House. I think she's got one due out soon. Surely Hector would like that, Sophie? He'd get people coming to his shop from miles around."

"The Cotswolds is a big region," I said hurriedly, resolving to change Minty's Twitter location to an untraceable 'English village' as soon as I got home. "She might be at the opposite end of the Cotswolds to us. She might not be willing to drive that far to sign a few books."

"She must earn enough to have a driver, or she could get a taxi," said Julia.

Dinah snorted. "I hardly think so. It's difficult enough even for a bestseller to make a living wage from writing these days, never mind afford a chauffeur."

"I wouldn't mind going to pick her up in my car if it would help," said Karen. "What a great opportunity for a one-to-one chat."

I played for time. "It would take an awful lot of planning."

"We once had a royal visit at a school where I used to work," said Julia. "It was run like a military campaign, with security officers and all sorts of red tape. But everyone agreed it was worth the hassle. It couldn't be any worse than that."

"It might help persuade her to come if we arranged for the local paper to send a photographer," said Bella. "Her publisher would probably appreciate a bit of local press coverage."

"Or we could make it into a whole-day event, with a VIP reception on her arrival," said Dinah. "We'd be the VIPS, along with Hector, of course, and we could get

Donald to lay on a special lunch at The Bluebird, before we bring her over to the shop for the actual book signing."

"Yes, you'll need Hector," I said faintly, sitting back in my seat, arms hanging limply by my sides.

"Can you fill him in with our ideas tomorrow, please, Sophie?" said Dinah. "He'll be more likely to cooperate if the suggestion comes from you."

Ticking the item off on her agenda, she moved on to the next item, as if Hermione Minty's visit was a done deal.

"Over my dead body," said Hector when I carried out Dinah's instructions in the shop the next afternoon.

"Where's a dead body?" said Tommy. "Who's died?" He looked up from the tearoom table where he was busy popping the bubbles on a sheet of bubble wrap that Hector had given him to distract him from 'helping' customers. Then he pulled his magnifying glass out of his pocket, ready to investigate.

"Figure of speech, Tommy," I said. I knew he wouldn't know what a figure of speech was, but I thought it might keep him out of the conversation. "We're talking about Hermione Minty."

"Is she dead, then?" asked Tommy.

"No, she's fine," I said quickly. "She's alive and well."

"Phew," said Tommy. "That's a relief. I don't want my mum upset."

He went back to popping bubbles.

Hector folded his arms. "I presume you said no?"

I looked away. "It would have seemed rude and defeatist to say no straight off. I want them to think it's the sort of thing that Hector's House could do in principle."

65

Hector sighed. "Well, of course we could do it in principle, but not with Hermione Minty. I should have thought that was obvious."

Tommy, all bubbled out, screwed up the flat plastic sheet and stuffed it in the tearoom's bin.

"I don't see what the problem is," he said. "Why don't you ask someone else? Like Jane Ostrich or Charlotte Pronto?"

Hector laughed. "Or how about Shakespeare? Thanks for the thought, Tommy, but they're all long dead."

"Really? I'd better break it gently to my mum, in case she likes them too. I don't think she's read any of their books, but we've got at least ten books in our house, so there's a good chance we might have something by one of them. So where does she live, then, this Hermione Minty?"

Hector and I looked at each other in silence, wondering how to answer.

"Round here somewhere, apparently," said a middle-aged lady, browsing the fiction section. She'd been so quiet I'd forgotten she was there.

"Really?" I said blankly, wondering where she'd got that from.

She replaced the novel and turned to address us more directly. "Yes, I'm sure I saw something on Facebook about it yesterday."

"I think you'll find it was on Twitter," I said, while Hector ducked out of the conversation by pretending to be busy with the order book. "But you know what these celebrity authors are like. They pop up everywhere. Always on the move. Book signings and launches and festivals and the like."

"What does she look like, this Minty person?" asked Tommy, wandering over to the central display table to

66

pick up one of her books. "I wonder whether I've ever seen her? Maybe I even know her already, but don't know her by name." He flipped the book over, then opened the front cover. "This is a rubbish book. It hasn't got her picture anywhere."

I tried not to look at Hector for fear of giving the game away.

"She might like to protect her privacy," I said. "It's hard for successful people to live normal lives if they've got everyone in the street recognising them every five minutes."

The lady in the fiction section nodded. "Yes, it must be awful for the Royal family, never being able to pop out to the shops or go to the park without having paparazzi after them."

Tommy perked up. "Paparazzi? Isn't that a sort of sausage?"

Hector sniggered. "You're thinking of pepperoni. Though paparazzi would be a good name for pepperoni pizza. You should ask Carol to stock it. It would be right up her street."

"I could just eat a pizza now," said Tommy, zipping up his Parka and heading for the door. "I'm going to the village shop to see if she's got any."

"That reminds me, I really came in to buy a diet book," said the lady, turning away from the novels. "New Year's resolutions, eh? Just over a week in, and I'm already falling off the wagon."

I knew the feeling.

When I walked home after work, Tommy was still lurking in the High Street, peering into all the parked cars in turn. As I approached him, he pulled his diary out of his pocket to write the registration number of a blue saloon.

"What are you doing, issuing a parking ticket?"

"Can I do that?" He sounded keen. "Is that like making a citizen's arrest?"

"No, I'm kidding. Only policemen and parking attendants can do that. Sorry to disappoint you."

Tommy shook his head. "Don't worry, I couldn't do it now, anyway. I'm on a case. I'm tracking down Hermione Minty. I think I might be hot on her trail."

I recoiled.

He pointed to the car's rear window. "See? There's a clue. There's one of her books on the parcel shelf."

Only when I let out a puff of air did I realise I'd been holding my breath.

"But that's the vicar's car. Don't you recognise it?"

Tommy stood back to appraise it. "Then why isn't it outside the vicarage?"

The vicarage was at the other end of the High Street.

"I don't know. He must be visiting someone. Maybe he was late for a meeting and jumped in the car to speed things up."

There were plenty of mornings when I wished I had a car to get me to work on time, even though Hector's House was only five minutes' walk from my cottage.

"The Reverend Murray." Tommy wrote the name in his diary. "I think his wife must be my number one suspect."

"His wife?" I was genuinely surprised. "Why his wife?"

Tommy looked at me like I was stupid.

"Because she's a woman, of course. Hermione's a girl's name. Honestly, don't you know anything, miss?"

I smiled. Tommy had clearly forgotten that I'd pointed this very same fact out to him a few days ago.

"You're right, Tommy. That's why you're the detective, and I work in a bookshop."

9 Angel Heart

Lying on my sofa after tea, toes towards the comforting glow of the wood-burning stove, I realised that reading Minty's books would help me tweet credibly on her behalf. Familiarising myself with her turn of phrase would enable me to mimic her way with words, so that her fans didn't think her social media was managed by a minion at her publishing house.

At least, that was my official justification for reading the books. I thought they might also explain why Hector was so keen to protect his anonymity. Perhaps they espoused a world-view of which he'd be ashamed, or revealed past secrets better kept hidden from the world. Tommy's obsession with detective work was catching.

I'd been going to sneak one of her books out of the shop that afternoon while Hector wasn't looking, despite the risk of a citizen's arrest for shoplifting if Tommy spotted me. Then I remembered that Auntie May had a shelf full of them in the cottage, given to her by Hector as a thank you for being his financial backer when he started the shop.

I braced myself to open the first of her books, *Angel Heart*, at the About the Author page. That was the only part of the book's interior that I'd ever read, and it told me nothing I didn't already know.

I flipped past the copyright page to the dedication: 'To Celeste'.

Despite her having left him some years before, he'd left this message in place for all the world to see. A wave of nausea washed over me. Perhaps all his books bore the same dedication. Perhaps this was why he'd never pressed them on me to read, as he'd done with so many others. I had no illusions that I might have usurped Celeste in his affections yet, as we had only been dating since the autumn, but it struck me as unnecessarily heartless to continue to fly the flag for her like this right in front of me, every day, in the shop.

I snapped the book shut without reading any further and threw it down on the coffee table, knocking my mug over and spilling my tea. I'd read more than enough.

The cheery knock on my front door was a welcome distraction from my misery. My unexpected visitor was the vicar, standing hunched in the doorway against the rain.

"Come in, vicar," I said warmly, feeling like a character from a farce. "What can I do for you this dark and stormy night?"

He slipped off his long, dark cloak, hung it on the hallstand, and followed me to the fireside, where he made himself comfortable on the sofa.

"I wanted to talk to you about your new role at Sunday School."

Inwardly I groaned, regretting my rash agreement, following the success of my nativity play before Christmas, to fill the vacancy for Sunday School teacher.

He held his damp hands towards the wood burner.

"So fortuitous that we should gain a trained teacher in the village who no longer works in a classroom," he continued. "All the skills and experience, with none of the daily grind."

I frowned. "I may be a trained teacher, but I'm pretty ignorant about the sort of thing you teach at Sunday School. We used to go to church when I was little, but I've fallen by the wayside since then."

He smiled. "Don't sell yourself short, Sophie. You're clearly sufficiently *au fait* with church jargon to use Christian analogies. We'll make a Sunday School teacher of you yet. It won't be that difficult. At this level, it's as much about storytelling as theology. And it only needs to be for an hour or so, including crafts, activities, snacks, a couple of songs and a prayer."

I opened my mouth to protest, but was cut short by the vicar suddenly gasping and starting a coughing fit. By the time I'd brought him a glass of water from the kitchen, he'd recovered enough to unwrap a sweet from a plastic packet in his jacket pocket. He offered the bag to me to take one for myself.

"Murray Mint, Sophie? I never travel without them. I use them as my calling card to help people remember my name." He seemed pleased to introduce someone new to his joke and warbled in a pleasant tenor, "'Murray Mints, Murray Mints, too good to hurry mints!'" He leaned towards me. "You're too young to remember the old advertisement, but its jingle used to be a useful chat-up line when I was a young man."

73

I wondered whether this was before or after he'd taken the cloth.

However, it would take more than a peppermint to convince me I was the right person to run a Sunday School class. "The thing is, vicar, I'm a bit tied up at the moment with other projects."

"On Sundays?"

I couldn't lie to a vicar. "No, but Sunday's my only day off."

In truth, I could have taken more days off during the week, but I wanted to spend as much time as possible with Hector. The vicar gave me a knowing look, which made me want to explain exactly what was keeping me so busy.

"Business in the bookshop has been really quiet since Christmas, so I'm doing extra work to help to keep it afloat," I said. "Plus Ella and I are helping Donald arrange a special Valentine's Night at The Bluebird, because he's also feeling the pinch."

The vicar raised the glass of water that I'd handed him.

"Never give two excuses when one will suffice. It's suspicious. But let's help each other however we can. Perhaps you might start at Easter?" He set the glass down on the coffee table. "Palm Sunday would be ideal. The live donkey parading down the High Street is a real draw for the children, who all want a turn at leading it. On Easter Sunday there will of course be a church tea with hot cross buns and Easter eggs, and a decorated bonnet contest."

"Isn't that a bit sexist?" I asked, picturing little girls in flower-trimmed straw hats.

"Good Lord, no," said the vicar. "Lots of boys join in, and quite right too. And the dads. It gets very competitive. I suspect the PTA runs a book on it, but if that's what it takes to get them into church, I'm prepared to curb my disapproval of gambling for once. Mysterious ways, and all that. So you have my blessing to get your Valentine's Day business out of the way first, and then we'll have a good run-up at it. Don't feel you're letting the side down, because Valentine was a Christian martyr."

"Valentine was a martyr? Gosh, yes, he must have been."

"In the meantime, you could practise for Sunday School by helping me raise awareness of the true meaning of Valentine's Day. I've written a little pamphlet about him. Perhaps Hector might like some for his shop window. He always sets up a good display of romantic novels for it."

I bet he does, I thought, and I know whose books will have pride of place.

"I can ask him. What exactly is the religious story behind it? I presume it's something romantic."

The vicar smiled ruefully. "Actually, like so many saints' tales, there are lots of alternatives. One of them is rather grim. The fourteenth of February is thought by some to mark the day that Saint Valentine was beheaded, back in two hundred and something AD, in the reign of a Roman emperor called Claudius the Cruel. Not the kind of name to endear you to your subjects. The emperor was having trouble recruiting into his army because men didn't want to leave their wives and children. He thought his existing forces would fight better if their womenfolk weren't, er, sapping their strength before they went into battle. A bit like footballers before a match, if you know what I mean. So he came up with an ingenious solution: he banned marriage."

I laughed. "He didn't think that one through. If he ruled long enough, he wouldn't have any men left at all, or women either."

The vicar smiled. "It was certainly no way for a society to conduct itself."

"So how did Valentine come into it?"

Reverend Murray got up to put another log on the fire for me, quite at home now.

"Well, my dear, Valentine was an old romantic after your own heart. He defied the emperor and continued to conduct marriages in secret. When Claudius found out, he was livid, and ordered Valentine's execution. The poor man was sentenced to be clubbed to death, and then have his head cut off."

"Ugh! That's not very romantic at all."

"While he was imprisoned awaiting his execution, he befriended the jailor's daughter. Legend has it that when he died, he left her a farewell note signed 'From your Valentine'."

"Gosh. And that was the last she saw of him."

"Yes."

We both sat in silence for a moment, sipping our drinks for comfort. I was first to speak.

"So if you ask someone to be your Valentine, you're effectively asking them if they'd like to be clubbed to death and have their heads cut off?"

The vicar nodded playfully. "According to that version of the legend, yes. You'd have to be really in love to say yes to that. But you see, my dear, I've just demonstrated the power of storytelling to convey a spiritual message. You'll never forget that tale now, will you? That's all I'm asking you to do with the children at Sunday School. I'll feed you the stories in advance."

To my surprise, I found myself relishing the prospect. "I think we'd better skip that version of the Valentine's story at Sunday School. We don't want the children re-enacting it in the playground next day."

The vicar laughed. "Indeed. The more important message is that people are meant to live together in partnership and harmony. We are greater than the sum of our parts, so to speak. But that doesn't mean I shan't be celebrating Valentine's Day with my dear wife in private. Beneath this dog collar, I am flesh and blood, you know."

He wiggled his eyebrows suggestively, making me giggle.

"'If you prick us, do we not bleed?'" I hoped this quote was an appropriate retort. Hector would have been proud of me. I think.

I moved us back on to less risqué territory.

"So will you be booking a table for two at The Bluebird's special Valentine's dinner?"

He beamed. "Most certainly. There are many more ways of worshipping God than going to church, and supporting local community events is one of them." I wondered whether he'd been into The Bluebird lately. "Like the saints, God is ever-present, every day of the year, whatever we do, wherever we go, and not only in church on Sundays." He delved in his pocket again. "Now, can I offer you another mint before I go?"

10 Cocoa Rush

After my last pupil of Wednesday afternoon had gone, and the shop had finally emptied of customers, I was glad to have the opportunity to sit down on the stool behind the trade counter for a rest while Hector was ferreting about in the stockroom, looking for a book he'd put in a safe place before Christmas and now couldn't find. I'd just settled down to read the latest edition of *The Bookseller* when a loud crash at the door startled me.

I half-expected to see a thug coming in to raid the till, but it was only Tommy, pushing the door so hard it rebounded from the rubber stop in the floor and came back to hit him on the shoulder. He appeared undaunted, though I suspected he'd find a bruise there by the morning.

"Got any odd jobs you want doing?" he asked hopefully.

For a moment I considered asking him to set the tea tables ready for the next morning, but that would have been like asking a bull to organise a china shop. I glanced around.

"You could tidy up the display table if you like."

Even Tommy couldn't break a book.

It took him a while to match the displaced books to the right piles, like a toddler puzzling over a shape sorter. Halfway through, he paused to sneeze loudly and dramatically, jogging the table and sending several piles of Minty books tumbling to the floor like Jenga bricks.

I got up to help him pick them up again.

"Wretched Minty!" I murmured.

Tommy paused to look at me quizzically. "You don't like that Minty person? I thought all ladies liked Hermione Minty."

I frowned. "Well, this lady doesn't. There are times when I could cheerfully strangle her."

Tommy straightened up, leaving me to gather the fallen books, pulled his diary out of his school blazer pocket and started to scribble in it. "Has cheerfully got one l or two?" he asked after a moment.

"What? Why?"

Tommy tapped the side of his nose with his pen, leaving behind a blob of black ink like a malignant freckle. "Just a precaution." I bet he didn't know the meaning of the word before he started reading his new detective skills book. "So where do you think Hermione Minty lives?"

I lined up the corners of the piles of books, grateful that Tommy's sneeze hadn't damaged them beyond saleability.

"I've no idea, Tommy. How would I know?"

Tommy shrugged. "I thought you famous writers might hang out together somewhere."

"Famous? Me? How do you work that out?"

"You write things and you're in that writing group. You all published a book together, so you must be famous."

He meant the little homespun Christmas anthology, gallantly turned into a printed book for the Wendlebury Writers by Hector. I suppose when you're fourteen and have only ever lived in one little village, fame is relative.

With a flourish, he finished writing his note and pocketed his diary and pen, not bothering to replace its cap. Ink immediately started wicking its way down towards the side seam.

"Although if you want to strangle her, it's probably just as well you don't know where she lives," he said.

I decided he needed a diversion.

"Go and ask Hector to let you flatten the empty cardboard book boxes and put them out for recycling. That'll be enough to earn you a mug of cocoa. I was about to make one for me and Hector anyway."

The sound of the kettle boiling and the clatter of mugs was not enough to drown out the noise of Tommy jumping on box after box in the stockroom. Hector emerged, probably for his own safety, as I was squirting clouds of whipped cream from an aerosol can on to three mugs of hot chocolate.

"I think Tommy's missed his vocation as a stunt man." Hector watched me crumble a small chocolate flake across the three little clouds, the bits sinking down like gravel in snow. "You know, the kind that use piles of cardboard boxes to break their fall."

He wrapped his hands round his mug for warmth. The stockroom radiator was always at a lower temperature than the ones in the shop to save on electricity. He pulled out a chair at the tearoom table and I sat beside him. Tommy joined us, slamming the stockroom door in his wake, before stirring four lumps of brown sugar into his cocoa. He guzzled it down quickly, then ran his index finger round the rim of the mug to capture the last few flakes of grated chocolate.

"Have you got anything else for me to do? I wouldn't mind earning a cake."

He glanced longingly at the cupcake stand. Wary of how much sugar he had already ingested, I was firm for once.

"This isn't a food bank, you know. You've done enough to earn your luxury hot chocolate, but that's all we've got for you today."

Tommy scraped his chair back. "OK, I'll try the village shop. They've usually got plenty of cakes left at the end of the day. Maybe Carol will have some odd jobs for me."

I knew Carol would be too kind-hearted to turn him away, so I tried to redirect his energies elsewhere.

"I tell you who does want some help, Tommy, and that's Donald. He's got loads of junk stashed in his courtyard to get rid of. Ask him if you can help shift it for him. I presume he'll be bagging it up so he can take it down to the recycling centre in Slate Green."

"Why doesn't he sling it all down that old well of his?"

Hector nodded. "Good point, Tommy. If Donald's going to get it filled in, why not use it as his own personal landfill site first? It'll save petrol and backache if he doesn't have to take all the stuff to the tip. Then when he pours in the concrete to seal the well, it'll trickle down between the cracks, saving him money on materials."

"Like the ice-cream melting in a sundae," I said thoughtfully, wondering whether I should add ice-cream sundaes to the tearoom menu in the summer. If Donald's new beer garden might compete with our tearoom, we'd need to up our game.

Tommy put his hands on his hips, oozing confidence. "I could do that for him. I'm good at flinging stuff down the well. I do it all the time. Thanks for the hot chocolate, miss."

With that, he made a boisterous exit, adding another dent to the wall. Hector got up to close the door Tommy had left open behind him, stopping the icy air gusting in from the High Street.

11 Beside the Seaside

I squinted against the razor-sharp sunshine. "Hector."

"That's me."

As we headed down the M5 motorway to visit Hector's parents the following Sunday, I took the opportunity to put a question to Hector that had been bothering me since Carol's birthday.

"I want to ask you something."

"I'm listening."

We'd left the gently rolling hills of the Cotswolds far behind, passing the big Cribbs Causeway retail park on the outskirts of Bristol, and were now descending steadily past the murky industrial sprawl of Avonmouth Docks. The Somerset Levels, the flat fields of that county, sparkled ahead of us in the distance beneath a brilliant cloudless sky. They looked like they'd been damped down ready for ironing. The long, straight drainage ditches dividing the fields struck me as slightly sinister, taunting farmers with a veiled threat of flooding. The fields looked eerily lifeless. I didn't know why. Then I put my finger on it. There wasn't a Cotswold sheep in sight. It felt as if we were plummeting into a whole different country.

"It's a bit sensitive," I said.

"So am I, so you've come to the right place. Go on, spit it out, whatever it is."

I took a deep breath. "Do you think it's ever justifiable to betray a confidence? If it is for the greater good of the person who has confided in you?"

He glanced over his shoulder, flipped the indicator, and moved out into the middle lane.

"You mean is it in the same league as a white lie? I suppose it depends on what that confidence is, and on the judgement of the person confided in."

I sighed. "Maybe I'd better tell you and you can decide."

I gave him a sideways glance to check his reaction, but his face was expressionless, his eyes on the road ahead. His silence made the sound of the road surface beneath the tyres preternaturally noisy. Then he sighed.

"If you don't tell me what it is after that build-up, I might assume something much worse. That's how rumours start."

I felt a wave of relief wash over me at the permission to unburden myself.

"The thing is, Bertie Thompson is threatening to return to Wendlebury. Carol told me he phoned her, hinting that he wants to make amends and start again."

A car to our right hooted as Hector inadvertently crossed the white line.

"Surely he can't be serious! He's about twenty-five years too late. Does he honestly think anyone will tolerate his presence in the village, even Carol? Or Billy? When he abandoned Carol, he severed all ties with his family. Never even came back for his parents' funerals."

"I hadn't considered Billy's position. What a trial siblings can be. It's at times like this that I'm glad I'm an only child, aren't you?"

Hector pursed his lips. "I wouldn't want a brother like Bertie, that's for sure. To be honest, I'd be very surprised if Bertie really did come back to Wendlebury Barrow after all this time. Even he can't be that thick-skinned. But if he does, we'll send him packing, one way or another."

As the sign for the Clevedon turn-off rose up on the horizon and Hector moved into the slow lane, my thoughts turned to meeting his parents. This was a big step for Hector as well as for me. He'd never introduced any girlfriends to them since Celeste left him.

As we circled the roundabout, corporation-planted with purples pansies, I remembered they'd barely seen Celeste either, although she and Hector had been together throughout university and a couple of years beyond. That struck me as strange for someone so close to his parents.

Maybe his mother was the sort who was desperate to marry him off and worried about him being left on the shelf. If so, he'd be scared she'd frighten girls off or give casual dates unhelpful hopes of marriage. Or maybe she was the sort who never thought any woman was good enough for her son, so would drive them away. Perhaps witnessing the rift between Carol and her parents had made her ultra-cautious.

We descended into the town centre and beyond.

"Do you ever wish you lived by the seaside?" I asked Hector as we got our first glimpse of the sea. "What a beautiful pier."

"That's the only Grade I listed pier in the country," he said proudly.

As we drove along the seafront, Hector cranked his window open a couple of inches to allow a waft of icy ozone to be sucked into the Land Rover.

"As approved by the Poet Laureate," Hector continued. "John Betjeman said it was the most beautiful pier in England, and he didn't praise architecture lightly. 'Come, friendly bombs, and fall on Slough. It isn't fit for humans now.'"

"That's a bit harsh," I said. "Poor Slough."

With its neat array of frilly old villas and cottages, Clevedon got my approval too, although the beach lacked the fine, light sands I was used to in Scotland. I gazed across the opaque brown water to the distant coast of South Wales. It didn't seem like real sea, either. On the wild coasts of north west Scotland, you could gaze westward, knowing that the next significant land mass was North America, bar the scattering of tiny Scottish islands whose history and culture my mother loved and had studied so much. Here the view stopped at Wales.

"I can see why my parents are happy here," said Hector. "It feels open and fresh. Not that we haven't got fresh air in the Cotswolds. Or does that sound silly?"

He shifted self-consciously in his seat as he flicked down the indicator to turn into the side street that I recognised as his parents' address.

"That's not silly at all. But I tell you what, if you like this, I'd love to show you the Scottish coast."

Hector smiled as he turned into the driveway of a neat bungalow just beyond the promenade. "Is that an offer, Sophie?"

My heartbeat quickened. I wasn't sure I was ready for him to meet my parents yet.

I gathered up my handbag, scarf, hat and gloves from the footwell, while Hector jumped down from his seat and came round to open the door for me. Taking me by the hand, he almost dragged me up the straight concrete path, past weedless flowerbeds dotted with the shoots of snowdrops and croci. With his own key, he let us in through the front door of his parents' bungalow.

I recognised Hector's parents instantly from the old photos that I'd found in his spare room when I was looking at his second-hand book collection before Christmas. I also vaguely remembered meeting them when I was a teenager, visiting their old antique shop with Auntie May one summer, when Hector was away at university. They were still sprightly and attractive, which made me think Hector would age well.

They recognised me too.

"Ah, those cheekbones!" said Nancy. "Edward, look at her cheekbones. Aren't they exactly like May's?"

I was glad she'd focused on my cheekbones and nothing more embarrassing.

"And the eyes. Your aunt was a beauty in her prime, Sophie." Edward gave a nod of approval to his son. I felt like a cow at the market, as if Hector had bought me for five magic beans.

Hector grabbed my hand again.

"Come on, Sophie, let me show you the garden. Sophie's keen on plants, Mum, like May."

He shoved me out into the kitchen and through the back door.

"I'm not that keen," I said when only he could hear. "Not in January. It's freezing out here."

"I'm just giving them time to talk about you while we're not in the same room. That and the fact I've brought a girl home."

"I'm not a girl, I'm a woman."

"You know what I mean. If it makes you feel any better, they still think of me as their little boy."

I bit back a smile. I was so used to seeing Hector in control in the shop, authoritative and wise, that it seemed odd to think of him being someone's little boy.

"By the time we go back in, my dad will have got the pre-lunch sherry out, and that'll make you relax."

"But I'm on the wagon."

"Please don't reject it. You'll only set him off on his standard lecture about the medical benefits of sherry."

He looked as dubious about that theory as I felt.

Hector led me by the hand around the long, narrow garden, his palm unusually damp. Immaculately weeded for the winter, the well-tilled, crumbly soil was disturbed only by the tops of narcissi planted in precise geometrical formations. Neatly espaliered apple trees spanned the wall at the bottom of the garden, looking as if someone had pressed them like flowers, then stood them upright for execution by firing squad. A ruthlessly manicured herb garden divided the lawn from the kitchen garden, which was spread with warming layers of compost ready for spring planting. Two tramlines of onions were the advance party of the summer's vegetable crop.

"It's very neat," I said at last.

Hector nodded. "I know. Dad likes a bit of order. The plants wouldn't dare not to grow under his management."

"I guess that's why you've turned out so tidy." I thought with shame of how neglected Auntie May's garden looked just now. I resolved to spend the next weekend turning over the soil and dressing it, ready for the spring. "I suppose I should be glad that it didn't send you in the opposite direction – wild and unruly."

When Hector scowled, I wondered whether I'd said something wrong, but before I could enquire, his mother appeared at the open back door to beckon us in.

"Hector, darling! Sophie! Drinkies!"

I smiled and waved to her to signal that we'd heard, and we started back up the garden path, me leading Hector this time.

While his mum bustled about in the kitchen putting the finishing touches to the Sunday lunch, Hector and his father engaged in conversation about Max Hastings' biography of Winston Churchill. As I'd not read the book in question, I couldn't comment, so contented myself with wandering around the room looking at the many ornaments and pictures, sipping viscous teak-coloured sherry from a delicate crystal schooner.

Regiments of photos paraded about the room in antique silver frames. Some of the images were vintage, too. Black and white prints had faded to sepia tones. Some went back to what looked like Victorian times, showing matching pairs of neat little children in sailor suits and long pinafores. The coloured photos of his parents' wedding and Hector's childhood seemed garish by comparison.

The extraordinary number of photos of Hector came as no surprise to me. Being an only child myself, I knew how easy it was for parents to go over the top. What struck me as odd was how much Hector's appearance had changed during his teenage years. He was Jekyll and Hyde, one moment with curls tumbling past his shoulders, embryonic dark beard shading his well-shaped chin; the next, his hair was short and neat and his face clean-shaven. In every picture there was the unmissable twinkle in his eye, but the longer the hair, the more outlandish the stance. Hector had always struck me as a modest dresser, apart from when wearing his fancy-dress toga at the village show, but in the long-haired pictures he was flamboyant, swaggering to the camera. This was not the Hector I knew.

I wondered whether there had been a tragedy in his childhood to make him change so dramatically. What might have triggered the transformation into the quiet man he was today? I set down a photo of him in the briefest of swimming trunks, about to dive off a cliff into what looked like Greek seas, long curls hanging down over his face as he headed for the sapphire waters below, and picked up another that appeared to have been taken on the same holiday. I stared at it in disbelief.

"But there's two of you here!" I said, hoarsely.

Hector and Edward, debating whether Churchill deserved his Nobel Prize for Literature (who knew?), didn't hear.

By some miracle, here were both versions of Hector together, sitting on a Greek beach, the short-haired one serious and sensible, the long-haired one pulling a face. Both Hectors looked about fifteen. I held the photo up to the window for more light. Both in jeans, they were differentiated by their t-shirts, sensible Hector's bearing a quote from Oscar Wilde in curling Art Nouveau lettering, and wild Hector's the photo of Che Guevara familiar from student bedroom walls.

"Dinner's ready, darlings," called Nancy, coming in to the room to round us up. Seeing me holding the photo, she came over to stand beside me, smiling proudly. "Of course, you haven't met Horace yet, have you, Sophie? Goodness, Horace practically lived in that Che Guevara top until his girlfriend of the moment adopted it. I've forgotten her name. Hector, darling, which was the one with spiky hair? When he broke up with her, he seemed to be sadder to lose the t-shirt than the girl. I was glad to see the back of both of them."

"Horace?" I echoed weakly, unable to get beyond her first sentence. "Who is Horace? Hector, why did you never tell me you had a brother?"

Hector scrutinised his sherry. "Didn't I?" he said, his air of innocence unconvincing.

Nancy put her hand on the back of my waist to usher me through to the dining room.

"Really, Hector? How remiss of you."

Hector and Edward followed behind us.

"There hasn't exactly been the opportunity to introduce them, Mum." I'd never heard him sound petulant before.

In the dining room, Edward pulled out a high-backed mahogany chair and beckoned me to sit down. I could see where Hector got his good manners. As Hector took his place opposite me, I glanced around the elegant table, vintage linen cloth, thinned by age, beneath gleaming antique silver cutlery, cruet and candelabra. A low silver rose bowl at the centre was filled with glossy sprigs of rosemary branches, their spiky dark leaves exuding an energising scent. Such a fine array of antiques seemed out of place in a modern bungalow, but his parents seemed to feel they had found the best of both worlds.

The linen-decked table, big enough for eight, was set for five.

Five?

"It's not as if Horace ever comes to visit us," Hector was saying to Nancy. "If at any point since I'd met her he'd deigned to be in the same country as us, of course I'd have introduced Sophie to him. Even the same hemisphere would help."

From the hallway came the sound of a key turning in the lock of the front door.

"Ah, but that's where you're wrong," said Nancy, setting down a dish of roast potatoes on a pewter trivet. There was a glimmer of triumph in her deep green eyes, so much like Hector's.

"Late again," said Edward, looking at the grandfather clock in the corner.

"In the dining room, darling!" Nancy called over her shoulder, as hasty, firm footsteps sounded across the tiled hall floor towards us.

"Surprise!" Suddenly in the doorway, larger than life, was a hairier, tanned, and more colourfully dressed version of Hector. "Hecate!" it cried, flinging its arms wide.

"Horatio!"

Surprised I certainly was, not least by their silly nicknames for each other. I glanced across the table to Hector, to check he wasn't playing a trick on me. No, he was still there, smiling a little awkwardly. Then I looked back to Horace, broad-chested inside his Bondi Beach sweatshirt above long shorts, bronzed, hairy legs, and well-worn hiking boots. I wondered whether this was how Hector had looked when he returned from hitchhiking in Africa with Celeste.

"For God's sake, Horace, it's the middle of winter!" Hector looked askance at Horace's outfit, but he got up from his seat to receive his twin's manly bear-hug.

"Not in Sydney, it isn't." Horace drew back from their embrace to stand, hands on hips, as comfortable as if basking in the southern hemisphere's sunshine. "And that's where I was until two days ago."

Hector turned to Nancy.

"Why didn't you forewarn me, Mum?"

Nancy tutted. "He only got back yesterday. Besides, I don't think forewarn is the right word to use, dear. And Horace thought it would be fun to surprise you."

"And who might this be?" said Horace, coming over to stand beside me. Sitting down, I felt at a disadvantage, but he clearly knew how to put a girl at her ease. In a swift, smooth and well-practised action, before I even realised what he was doing, he'd picked up my right hand and pressed it against his lips.

"Enchanted, sweetheart." Smiling with not a little self-satisfaction, he nodded to his brother. "Good work, Hector." He walked round behind the table to take the place set next to Hector. The contrast between them was remarkable. Hector could have been Horace's ghost. "Now, aren't you going to introduce us properly?"

Hector sighed. "As I'm sure Mum and Dad must already have told you, this is Sophie Sayers, my girlfriend and colleague." At least he was getting that description in my preferred order these days. "She lives in Wendlebury."

Horace raised his eyebrows hopefully. "With you?"

"No, she has her own cottage. You know, May Sayers' old place. But she works in the shop with me."

Horace freed his napkin from its silver filigree ring, shook it vigorously and spread it across his strong thighs.

"Well, you know what I'm always telling you, Hector, all work and no play—" He gave me a stagey wink, and I giggled before I could stop myself.

"So you're the expert on work, now, are you, Horace?" Hector said mildly. "Well, that's good news."

Horace slapped one hand down on the table, making the cutlery jangle. He wasn't being aggressive; he was just strong.

"Leading tourists round the outback is hardly a walk in the park. And it beats being stuck indoors all day, though I guess that keeps you out of the rain, wind and snow of Wendlebury Barrow."

I had a sudden thought. "Hang on, why didn't Hector's godmother, Kate, mention you when she came back from her visit to Australia in November? Didn't she see you?"

Instantly I regretted speaking in case I was stirring up some secret family feud.

Horace turned his green-eyed gaze on me. It was hard to believe he was not Hector in an unruly wig and spray tan.

"It was precisely because I wasn't there that she was able to stay so long. She borrowed my flat while I was off on a long expedition in New Zealand. I'd planned to see her before she went back, but my party got lost in the bush for five days, and we missed our flight back. So Kate and I missed each other by about a week. Strewth!"

Nancy gave a little gasp of horror. I suspected this was the first she'd heard of the danger he'd been in. Horace quickly diverted the conversation to me instead.

"Ever been to Oz, Sophie?"

"No, never."

"You don't know what you're missing, babe. If you ever fancy stepping out for a little adventure down under, you must look me up." He pulled out of one of the many pockets in his shorts a shiny business card, with a photo of a koala bear on one side, and his name, email and social media addresses on the other. No postal address, I noticed. I guessed he was always on the move – and that he always had one of these cards handy to back up his chat-up line to women, as well as to hand out to potential clients.

"Oh, he's adorable!" I stroked the image of the little koala with my forefinger, smiling at the outsized nose and fluffy ears. "Do you know, Horace, when I was little, my favourite toy was a koala? I called him Kenny. He was ever so cuddly."

Horace leaned towards me until his face was inches from mine. He was close enough for me to smell his cologne. Would one wear cologne in the outback? Perhaps it was his natural scent. He spoke in a low, intimate voice.

"You're never too old to cuddle a koala, Sophie."

"Oh dear God," said Hector, his hands over his eyes.

"Ah yes, let's say grace," said Edward quickly, either to defuse the sibling rivalry, or because that's what they always did before Sunday lunch. Obediently we bent our heads in prayer. Assuming everyone else would have their eyes closed, I peeked across at Horace, only to find him staring and smiling at me in a none-too-brotherly way.

I didn't dare look at Hector.

12 Brotherly Love

"Who's a pretty boy, then?"

I kicked myself for not turning off the talking parrot ringtone that I'd set to alert me to direct messages on Hermione Minty's Twitter account.

"Sorry." I reached across to the coffee table for my handbag, pulled out my phone and silenced it, but it had already interrupted our post-dinner conversation about Scotland. Hector, sitting next to me on the sofa, got up to refill our cups from the pot on the table.

"We need more milk, Mum," said Horace languidly, watching his brother drain the jug into my cup.

Nancy was sitting back in the armchair nearest the window with her eyes closed, recovering from serving us a delicious traditional Sunday roast dinner. "In the fridge," she said, pointing towards the door. Hector took the empty jug out to the kitchen to refill it.

Horace leapt up to take Hector's place, slipping his arm along the back of the sofa behind me. To move away from him without seeming rude, I leaned forward, as if simply intent on doing something tricky on my phone.

He looked over my shoulder as I logged in to Minty's account to check the message. "Ah, Twitter. When you're off in the outback as much as I am, you don't waste time on nonsense like that. We're too busy with real life to mess about with social media. We keep our satellite phones for serious use."

He read the screen. "I thought your name was Sophie? Who's Hermione? You're not dating my brother under a false identity, are you? Or hacking into someone else's account?"

"No, just following someone," I said hastily, jabbing at my phone to return to the home screen.

"Hermione Granger?" said Nancy, sitting bolt upright, her eyes snapping open as Hector returned to the room, milk jug in hand. "Oh yes, that dear girl in Harry Potter. Such a pretty thing; such presence on screen for one so young."

Hermione Granger? What did she have to do with anything?

Nancy shot a warning glance at Hector, then, seeing me watching her, gave me a scarcely perceptible shake of her head. So Horace didn't know about Hector's *alter ego*.

"Emma Watson, Mum, you mean Emma Watson," said Hector quickly.

I looked from Nancy to Hector and fell in with their ploy. "Ah yes, Emma Watson, I really admire her," I said. "She's such a great role model for young women and girls in real life, too." Nancy was looking relieved. "She's possibly my favourite actress," I added, although she wasn't.

"That Harry Potter is more versatile than one might expect of a lad who's grown up playing the same role over and over," said Edward, setting down his empty coffee cup. "What was the name of that Russian doctor he played in that television series we watched at Christmas? You know, the really dark one?" He watched Hector put

100

the jug down carefully on its coaster. "Hector, you'll know. The Russian doctor that Harry Potter played. Ends up on morphine."

Hector considered. "A *Young Doctor's Notebook*, based on the short stories by Mikhail Bulgakov. And it's Daniel Radcliffe, Dad, not Harry Potter."

He jerked his head to direct Horace to move from his seat. Horace stood up and stretched with the languor of a lion that's just finished digesting an antelope.

"I'm off for a swim in the sea. Who's joining me? Sophie?"

Nancy sat back and closed her eyes again. "Don't you think it's a little soon after your lunch, dear?"

"Nah. Cramp is for wimps."

A flicker of anxiety crossed her face.

I was genuinely curious. "Aren't you worried about how cold and muddy the sea will be? I don't suppose the waters of the Severn Estuary could be much more different from the Australian Pacific."

Horace grinned and flexed his arm muscles.

"They're what made me the man I am today."

He headed out of the room.

"Don't be too long, love," Nancy called after the closed door.

My eyes widened. "How far is he going to swim?"

Edward tutted. "As far as The Moon and Sixpence. That's a pub at the far end of the seafront."

I smiled. "I didn't think you meant the Somerset Maugham novel." I'd borrowed a copy of that from Hector's second-hand stock, attracted by the whimsical title. Hector looked impressed.

"Don't believe Horace's bluster, Sophie," Edward continued. "He is what he says, a wilderness tour guide, but he's not that reckless. Funnily enough, Hector was the more adventurous when they were boys."

"Still, he's having fun, and if both my boys are happy, I'm happy." Nancy smiled sweetly at Hector, who almost purred at his mother's approval. Then, invigorated by her post-lunch rest, she slapped her hands down on the arms of her chair and sprang to her feet. "So, everyone ready to hit the car boot sale?"

"Car boot sale," said Hector, and he went to fetch our coats.

When we got back to the bungalow, carrying a big bag of second-hand books, we found Horace sitting with his feet up on the coffee table watching the rugby, a bottle of beer in his hand. Hector pulled out our star purchase to show his brother.

"You see, 'there are more things in heaven and earth, Horatio, than are dreamt of in your philosophy'. Ah, that never gets old."

"And it never gets funny, either," said Horace evenly, but he took the small, faded hardback from Hector to look at. "Strewth! What language is this in? Welsh?"

"Gaelic," I said proudly. "My mum will love it. She lectures in Scottish History and Culture at the university in Inverness, and she's always on the lookout for vintage Gaelic books. Hector spotted this one beneath a heap of old books about salmon fishing. I got one of those for my dad, as he's into fishing, but my mum will be especially interested in this book as it's got a lengthy handwritten inscription in Gaelic, and a date on it. It might turn out to be a really rare book of great value, and Hector bought it for 20p. He's brilliant."

I flashed an appreciative smile at Hector, hoping Horace would have got the message by now that my affections lay firmly with his brother.

"A chip off the old block," said Edward contentedly.

"What, you mean pleasing women?" Horace winked at me.

"Oh Horace, you know what he means!" Nancy wagged a finger at him. "How to spot a good buy in a sale." She turned to me. "Your parents sound very interesting. I wonder whether I'll meet them one day."

"You've already met them at May's funeral," said Hector, rebuttoning his coat.

"Not stopping for a cup of tea before you head back to Wendlebury, dear?" asked Nancy.

"No, thanks, Mum, I'd rather do at least part of the journey in daylight."

"In the bush, we don't even have the streetlights to guide us." Horace gazed at me, wide-eyed. "Nothing but the stars, Sophie, and you should see the stars down under! It's like a whole different galaxy."

I smiled. "I should love to see them one day," I said truthfully, getting up and collecting my handbag from the coffee table.

Horace picked my phone up from the arm of the sofa and held it out to me. "Here you go, babe. I found it lying here when I got back from the pub. It kept making that crazy parrot noise. But don't worry, I've kept it safe for you." As he pressed it into my hand, one of his fingers tickled my palm. Now he was making fun of me. I drew back quickly.

"You didn't swim very far, then?" I wanted to make it clear his tricks didn't fool me for a moment.

"Only to the bottom of a couple of pints. Then I got bored and thought I'd better come back and see a bit more of Hector while he was down here, before I shoot off back to Australia. And a bit more of you, Sophie, of course."

His smile was awfully winning, like Hector's, but without the quiet modesty that made me feel safe.

"Off again so soon?" asked Hector. "You should have come a bit earlier to be here for Christmas."

"That's what I said, dear," said Nancy. "But you couldn't get away, Horace, could you?"

"Nope," said Horace. "And in any case, there was no point in paying for my own return fare when I knew this freebie was coming up. A free flight from Australia is worth waiting for."

"How did you swing a free trip?" I asked.

"I was a paid escort for this guy who'd been on one of my bush safaris. He's a nervous flyer and prefers not to travel unaccompanied. Billionaire rich, so I got to fly first class. He was only prepared to pay for me to fly tourist class back, so I'm hanging on for the cheapest late booking I can find, once I've had enough of the British winter. I don't mind missing a few days of an Australian summer, but I'll be glad to get back to it."

He slipped a smartphone out of the side pocket of his shorts and slid his thumb across the screen to check for messages. "Nah, nothing from the airlines yet. You've got me for a few more days, I think, Mum."

It must be hard to have a child living on the other side of the planet. I felt bad enough being at the far end of our small country from my parents. I didn't visit them as often as I should, although the flight from Bristol to Inverness was relatively cheap and only took about an hour. Seeing the pleasure on Nancy's face, I resolved not to leave it too long before I visited my own parents in Inverness, with or without Hector in tow.

"I don't suppose you'll have time to fit in a visit to Wendlebury Barrow before you go?" I asked. Hector shot me a dubious look. "Haven't you got friends there who'd like to see you?"

Horace nodded at Hector. "He's just seen me. The rest of my old Wendlebury friends have moved away to better things. Or at least to places where they can afford to live on their own salaries, rather than lodging for ever with their parents. They might come back when they've hit middle-age and the urge to settle down, get a job in a bank, and grow dahlias."

"Like Henry Pulling." I smiled, recognising his allusion to Graham Greene's *Travels with my Aunt*, the first book that Hector had given me. Perhaps there was more to Horace than Crocodile Dundee after all.

"Or open a bookshop." Horace winked at me.

Hector ignored the bait. "We'd better get going, Sophie, or we'll get caught in the Sunday night traffic jams."

He bent down to kiss his mother on the cheek, and she flung her arms round him and held him for a moment. Then his father came over to give him a manly pat on the back, and we headed for the door.

"Thank you for having me, Nancy, Edward," I said, pulling on my mittens. "It was a pleasure to meet you."

"The pleasure's all ours, dear," said Nancy. "Come again soon."

"Not a little of the pleasure was mine," added Horace in a low voice behind me, his warm hands briefly coming to rest gently on my shoulders, as I followed Hector out into the entrance hall. I took a final look at his long curls and his big green eyes, so reminiscent of Hector, yet so very different.

"Bon voyage, Horace," I said lightly, reaching up to give him a sisterly peck on the cheek, then trotted down the path to where Horace was already waiting for me in the Land Rover, engine running.

"How come no-one in the village has ever mentioned Horace to me? Is he some kind of black sheep who's been drummed out of Wendlebury?"

It was easier to ask Hector once we were on the motorway, staring at the lights ahead of us in the queue of traffic. It's always easier to ask tricky questions in a car, when you're isolated and intimate but can't make eye contact.

Hector smiled slightly at the second question. "No, he's all right. He's just been abroad for years, and, like he said, all his village mates have long since moved away. There's no reason for him to come back to Wendlebury since Mum and Dad moved to Clevedon. He's in a different orbit now."

"Apart from you," I said, trying to gauge his reaction out of the corner of my eye. "Do I take it Horace doesn't know about Hermione Minty?"

He shifted down into second gear as the traffic slowed up the hill. I looked back over my shoulder at the vast, flat expanse of fields behind us, twinkling in the late afternoon sunshine. Fleetingly I wished we could turn round at the next junction and head back down south, to find another quiet little seaside resort and take a break there, away from the village, away from his family, all by ourselves. We'd never been away together as a couple before.

"No, not even Dad knows about Minty. Only Mum. And Horace the He-man is the last person I'd want to know. He'd never take her books – my books – seriously.

As it is, he makes fun of her without even knowing she's me, reading aloud from Mum's copies of the books in a silly high-pitched voice that he's developed especially for the purpose. Can you imagine what he'd be like if he knew I wrote those books? He'd have a field day."

As the traffic slowed to a halt, Hector changed into neutral and applied the handbrake.

"Not that it matters to me as a writer. I mean, he's hardly my target audience, and I believe what I write is good stuff of its kind. I just don't want to have his voice in my head, teasing me as I write each new book. It may sound pretentious, but he'd kill my muse. Catch it and keep it in his crocodile trap. I don't want him to put me off."

I could see what he meant. "What sort of books does Horace read?"

"He doesn't. He prefers real life to books."

Now that the sun had gone down and there was no cloud cover, the cold was descending. Hector flicked a switch on the dashboard to turn on the heating.

"That's one reason he's living in Australia now – the availability of rugged sports and adventure all year round."

He said 'rugged sports' as if it was a perversion.

"Does he have a steady girlfriend?"

"He has girlfriends all right." Hector's face turned grim. "Very often someone else's."

I wondered whether that had included Celeste. Perhaps what Hector had told me about Celeste leaving him for another woman was a smokescreen. Supposing she'd left him for Horace, and that's why he'd moved to Australia – to be with her? I tried to dismiss the idea. If it were true, Hector would tell me when he was ready.

"Yet your dad said you were the sporty one when you were little."

Hector nodded, wiping condensation from the windscreen with a cloth, before handing it to me to do my side.

"Yes, until Horace became ill. Or rather, until he got better."

Hector seemed dogged by poorly people. He'd nursed Celeste through serious illness before she left.

"I'm the elder brother by a couple of hours. Usually twins are born in quick succession, but while my delivery was straightforward, Horace's birth was slow and complicated. He was always a little smaller and weaker than I was. Whatever bug I caught, he'd have it worse – and extra things that I didn't catch, too. Then when he was about eight, he was diagnosed with a childhood form of leukaemia." He took a deep breath. Although that was over twenty years ago, it clearly still pained him to talk about it. "For several years, he had a terrible time, with a barrage of treatments, until finally getting the all-clear."

"I'm so sorry. I'd never have guessed from looking at him now."

"Exactly. And all credit to Horace. As soon as he was back on form, he determined to build up his body as much as he could through stringent exercise programmes, attention to diet, and so on. He wanted to be the picture of health. His quest for constant sunshine and the outdoor life is all a part of that."

"I can see how someone in his position would feel that way." I felt in my coat pocket for a packet of mints and offered one to Hector before taking one myself.

"We'd always been close before, sharing everything, but when he became so ill, the whole dynamic between us changed – like he'd suddenly become my younger, fragile brother whom I constantly had to protect. Mum and Dad thought he could do no wrong. Or at least, they didn't like to tell him off when he was naughty, because they welcomed any display of high spirits or rebelliousness as indicators of his recovery."

"So his illness made him more flippant, but you more serious?"

Hector nodded. "I hadn't thought of it that way before, but I think you're right."

"And Horace plays on that?"

"He takes advantage of it. Mum and Dad still overindulge him. But then, wouldn't you, if that happened to our child?"

Startled, I flushed, wondering whether he realised he'd said "our child" not "your child". Suddenly things were moving faster than I was ready for. I crunched down on my sweet as he put the Land Rover into gear, released the handbrake, and the queue of traffic started to move.

13 Twin Peek

After our eventful Sunday, I was ready to spend the next evening quietly at home alone. I'd just settled down with a cup of tea and a good book when there was a hearty rap at the front door. I got up from the sofa to heave open the door, which was sticking a bit in the cold, damp weather.

"Hello, Horace, what a lovely surprise!"

I looked behind him, assuming Hector would be there too, but he was unaccompanied.

"That's a warm welcome for a cold, dark night," said Horace, grinning. "Thanks."

He strode into the hallway, pulling off his bush hat, and shook his long curls out like the 'after' image in a shampoo advert. Or maybe an advert for dog shampoo.

"What are you doing here?" I asked, closing the front door behind him. "How did you know where I lived?"

"Hector said you were living in old Miss Sayers' place. I used to play in her garden sometimes when I was a little boy. Till I got told off by the old man next door. He made me promise to come back only when she was there after that, rather than when she was off travelling."

"Did Hector used to come with you?"

"Of course. We were inseparable. One of the advantages of being a twin when you're a kid: you have a ready-made playmate."

"Why isn't Hector with you now?"

"I was going to ask you the very same thing. He's not at his flat, either."

"Oh, no, of course, I forgot. He's at a council meeting at Slate Green Library tonight. He advises its buyer about new books and local reading trends, to help him manage library stock."

Horace looked past me to the sofa. Taking the hint, I waved my hand towards it, realising this was no flying visit. If he'd come all the way from Clevedon, he'd want to sit down and relax for a bit.

"That sounds like a barrel of laughs."

I smiled conspiratorially. "I know. I usually volunteer to go with him for school visits, but council meetings are not my cup of tea at all."

Horace rearranged the scatter cushions around him, leaving enough space for me to sit beside him.

"Did you say tea?"

"I can take a hint."

"Milk, no sugar for me, sweetheart."

As I boiled the kettle, I wondered what Horace's intentions were. Why hadn't he phoned ahead to check that Hector would be at home? Or did he assume his brother had no social life?

I returned to set two mugs on the coffee table, one near Horace's knee, which thankfully was covered with proper trousers now, albeit the trekking kind with a zip to convert them into shorts at a moment's notice. I supposed Horace's knees would be much the same as Hector's. There can't be many women whose first sight of their boyfriend's bare legs is in a toga, though of

112

course, when I saw Hector in his Homer costume at the village show, he hadn't yet become my boyfriend.

Avoiding the cosy space Horace had cleared beside him, I settled down opposite, curling my legs under me in the ancient, overstuffed armchair.

"Mum's been telling me all about you," he said after taking a swig from his tea.

"How much can she know? Sunday was the first time she met me properly."

"You think Hector hadn't told her anything before your visit?"

I felt a little flutter of gratification inside.

"I've come to check you out further."

Was this some kind of chat-up line? "So you did know Hector wasn't going to be here!"

He gave an apologetic smile. "Guilty as charged."

This was awkward. How on earth was I going to avoid letting on to Hector tomorrow? Or could I just not tell him? Tangled webs, I cautioned myself.

"I thought we should get to know each other better while I'm over here," Horace was saying breezily. "We may not get another chance for a year or so." He set down his mug and leaned forward. "I'm the kind of guy who likes to seize the day. To make the most of opportunities as they arise."

I sat up straight, trying to look prim. I didn't have to try very hard.

"I'm sorry, Horace, I'm strictly a one-man girl." My voice was hoarse despite the tea. "I'm not sure you should have come."

Horace fell back in his seat, slapping his thighs and laughing.

"Congratulations, you've passed the test!"

I blushed. "Whatever do you mean?"

He straightened his face. "I'm certainly not coming on to you, honey, if that's what you're thinking. Not that I wouldn't if you weren't already taken. Don't get me wrong. You're a lovely girl. I just wanted to get to know you a little myself, without Hector there to speak for you or to protect you in any way. You know, Hector is a good brother to me. When I was a sickly kid, he always looked out for me. Now it's my turn to look out for him." He took another mouthful of tea. "That's not the easiest thing to do from the other side of the planet. But I need to make sure he doesn't get himself tangled up with the wrong kind of girl again. Not after that fiasco with bloody Celeste. He must have told you about Celeste."

I wasn't sure where this was going, so I trod cautiously. "Yes, a little. Enough for me to gather that she broke his heart, and made him wary of starting another serious relationship for a long time."

"Yes, the little bitch."

"The little…?" This was good news indeed. "You didn't like her?"

"God no, she was a witch. I mean, not in looks. Physically, she was stunning." That was something I didn't need to hear. "But she was incredibly selfish and manipulative. She made him take a gap year with her when he was keen to go straight into his Master's degree. He never wanted to go travelling at all, not beyond a normal holiday, but she gave him an ultimatum: her or his studies. Then she made him take her to outlandishly unsafe places. And when I say they're unsafe, you can take it from me they're death-traps. My tolerance of rough conditions is higher than most people's, but even I feared for his safety on that trip."

I thought of the crocodiles and snakes and spiders and burning heat and remorseless drought of the Australian

114

bush and shuddered. Celeste and Hector had planned to hitch-hike to Africa before she became too ill to travel. They made my European travels seem like a stroll down Wendlebury High Street.

"She didn't take her claws out of him even when she was ill. She monopolised him, trying to stop him leaving her alone even for a day trip to visit Mum and Dad. I called in to their flat a few times after she'd got better, to catch up with my big brother, and once when he was out, she started to flirt outrageously with me."

"But – but you just tried to flirt with me."

He shook his head. "Quite the opposite. I was testing you to make sure you hadn't set the same trap. Because trap it certainly was. Honestly, I don't know where it would have ended if I hadn't made a swift exit. Well, I do, but I couldn't have done that to Hector, and I don't know what made her think I might. Power games, I suppose."

He paused for a sip of his tea. "When she finally dumped him for that weird medic bird she ran off with, I did not mourn her departure for a moment. What a piece of work."

He leaned forward confidentially. "She was a real gold-digger. It's my theory that when she learned our parents were antique dealers, she assumed Hector must have been wealthy. If she'd bothered to come down to meet them sooner, she'd have taken one look at the shop and moved on."

"Gosh." My head was spinning like an overloaded washing machine.

"He never really saw it. Still doesn't. So you can see why I'm glad he's met you and is finally getting back into the saddle." I wasn't sure what to make of that analogy. "Thinking with his brain again instead of with his—"

I clattered the empty mugs together to take them out to the kitchen.

Horace called after me, "I don't think I could have held out without a woman for so long."

I bet he didn't have to, either, guiding willing tourists on dangerous treks. It would be all too easy for a girl to cling on to him at the sight of a snake on the pretext of being scared, and for him to offer as much comfort as she was prepared to accept. But Hector had misjudged Horace if he thought his brother was a borrower of other men's girlfriends. Horace seemed pretty decent to me.

I returned from the kitchen to find him picking up the book by Hermione Minty. I'd left *Angel Heart* face down on the coffee table, intending to tackle it again later, and had forgotten it was there until now.

"I'd have thought you were above stuff like this. Who's it by, anyway?" He turned the book over to look at the front cover. "Hermione Minty. What a name! Mum reads her books too, God knows why."

As I curled up again in the armchair, he opened it at random and read a description aloud in a high-pitched, mocking voice.

"'Her long curls were not so much twenty-four carat gold as rose gold, the kind favoured by legendary princesses, a precious blend of pure gold, silver and copper, spun together with love in mind to create a rarer beauty'. Well, talk of the devil! Cut through all that flowery nonsense, and you have the very image of Celeste." I froze. "That's the kind of weird hair colour she had. Mum swore it came out of a bottle. Several bottles, probably. High maintenance. Not a natural looker like you, Sophie."

He flashed his green eyes winningly. At last, a proper compliment. But I didn't let it distract me from a stout defence of Hermione Minty.

"She's really popular in our shop. Our local writers' group is desperate for me to get her to come in for an author visit. It would boost our takings, especially at this lean time of year, but—" I hesitated, choosing my words carefully "—for reasons too complicated to explain, there's no way we'll be able to arrange that."

He turned back to the book to read the "About the author" bit, but stopped before he got there at the dedication page. Beneath the printed dedication was a handwritten thank you from Hector to May. Horace read that aloud.

"Ah, sweet," he said, then stopped short, holding the page up for me to see. "But Jeez, have you seen the printed dedication: 'To Celeste.'" He lowered the book for a minute and stared at me. "There aren't many girls called Celeste. Does this mean what I think it means? Could this really be dedicated to Hector's Celeste? In which case, are Hermione and Hector one and the same?" Spotting my guilty expression, he threw back his head in a laugh that rippled all the way down his six-pack. "Strewth! I've got a sister and I didn't know it! All along I thought we were twins, when really we're triplets." He closed the book and hugged it to his chest. "Sweetheart, this is priceless!"

I couldn't help but laugh, torn between my promise of secrecy to Hector and Horace's infectious sense of fun. I ran my finger and thumb across my lips as if zipping them closed.

"Please don't ask. I'm saying nothing."

His laughter subsided into a roguish smile. "Why hasn't anyone else in the village sussed out his *alter ego*?

No, wait, I know – the little minx would never deign to visit him down here. Not posh enough for her. That's her loss, not Wendlebury's." He chewed his lip thoughtfully. "So Hector doesn't want me to know either, eh? I'm not surprised. He knows what a lark I could have with this. This joke could run and run." He turned serious for a moment. "I hope his adoring readers are paying him lots of dosh for his efforts."

"He does OK, but he doesn't earn as much as he could if we really promoted the books. That's why I set up a Twitter account for Hermione Minty. You saw me logging into it on Sunday. I wasn't following her. I was tweeting for her. I'm trying to raise her profile, to help him sell more books."

Horace looked doubtful. "If I've learned anything from my commercial ventures down under, it's that you have to make a big splash to be heard above the crowd of also-rans. You need to get other people to talk about her. It's no good tweeting alone in the jungle of noise out there." He paused to flick through the book again. "What you want is a big publicity stunt – in real life, not online. Where I work, we do that kind of thing all the time to draw attention to our tours."

"What, like wrestling crocodiles?" I could picture him doing that.

"To be more honest, it's more like taking tame wombats to tourist hotspots as a talking point. The ladies can't resist coming up to give them a cuddle, and then's our chance to chat them up and sell them tickets for our bush safaris."

I scratched my head thoughtfully. "I'm not sure we've got a match for wombats in Wendlebury. I don't think Billy's ferrets would have the same appeal."

Horace held the book by its chunky spine and flicked through the four hundred pages. "Phew, I wish I had Hector's staying power. And his brains. I don't know where he finds the time, working six days a week in the shop. And he must have written loads. Mum seems to have dozens of books by her – by him."

I smiled modestly. "That's why he hired me – to buy him more time to write while I do the donkey work in the shop."

"Well, if he's going to hire a donkey, he might as well hire one that's sweet and pretty."

"Aren't all donkeys?" I said playfully, then hoped he didn't think I was flirting.

He laughed. "And thank you for not wanting to tell me his secret. You're a good woman, Sophie, and that's what Hector's long deserved."

He put the book back on the coffee table and set his hands on his knees with the self-satisfied posture of someone who has achieved his objective.

"So, not only have you managed to resist my charms," he said cheerfully, "but as a bonus, you've demonstrated to me how much you care for my big brother."

"Actually I think you're bigger than him," I said, reaching out to touch one of Horace's bulging forearms. "I mean, you must get a lot more exercise and outdoor activity, to build your muscles up. Not that his muscles don't get a good work-out lifting boxes of books." I didn't want to sound as if I was putting Hector down.

Horace suppressed a smile as he stood up, ready to go now he'd accomplished his mission.

"Size isn't everything, sweetheart. Now you take care of my brother, or you'll have me to answer to next time I'm home."

14 Mint Condition

"I've cracked it, miss," said Tommy, flinging open the shop door so it crashed against the wall. "It's the vicar."

"What's the vicar?"

Hector didn't look up from his keyboard. "The vicar, in the crypt, with the thurible."

"What's a thurible?" I asked him.

"Liturgical incense burner," he replied. "Long metal ball on a chain. Not that they go in for that sort of thing much at St Bride's."

"That would make a great weapon," said Tommy cheerily, "if you swung it round your head a few times, like a bold knight with one of those spikey balls on a stick."

"But WHAT is the vicar?" My curiosity had been aroused.

"Oh, Herbie Tony Minty," said Tommy. "I think he's that Minty person. He gave me his code to let me in on the secret."

Hector looked up. "The vicar's got a secret handshake? That's news to me."

If there was a freemason's lodge in the village, I wondered who would be the grand master. Apparently not Hector, unless this was a double bluff.

"Who said anything about secret handshakes?" Tommy looked disappointed that he might have missed out on one. "I'm talking about sweets. The vicar gave me a mint sweet in a wrapper. And when he gave it to me, he said, 'It's distinctly Minty.'"

He slumped down on a tearoom chair as if the strain of receiving his coded message had exhausted him. "I don't think it could get any clearer than that, do you?"

"About as clear as a stick of peppermint rock, Tommy. He told me the other night that the reason he gives out mints is to make people remember his name."

"Yes, Minty."

"No, Murray. Didn't you read the packet the sweets came in? They're called Murray Mints. Murray is the brand name."

Crestfallen, Tommy pulled his diary out of his pocket and turned to a page filled with a scrawled list of mostly crossed-out names. He put a line through another one.

"I'd better keep looking," he said sadly. Stuffing the diary back in his pocket, he trudged out of the shop into the grey and drizzly High Street, little knowing that every step put more distance between himself and the real Hermione Minty.

Just then, a vaguely familiar green Mini went past the shop, the driver going so slowly as to be almost kerb-crawling. Tommy let out a yell and came running back to the shop, put his head round the door, and shouted to Hector and me.

"That was Hermione Minty in that car!"

"What?"

"Didn't you see the number plate? Who else round here would have a number plate saying M1 NTY?"

Before we could reply, he'd run off down the street, gaining on the car that was now dawdling past the school. I stood outside the shop door to see what he would do next. As he reached the car and banged on the passenger's window, the driver unaccountably put a spurt on, and with a crash of gears accelerated far beyond the speed limit, heading straight out of the village again.

I turned to Hector. "Do you know anyone who's got a green Mini?"

"Yes, but that's not her driving style," he said, getting up from behind the counter and coming out to join me in the street. "That was the driving style of someone completely different." He pursed his lips.

Suddenly the Mini came back into view, driving towards us, this time at full speed, until it screeched to a halt outside Hector's House. It veered sharply across the road and turned ninety degrees to park in front of Hector's Land Rover on the hardstanding beside the shop. The personalised number plate was precisely level with the shopfront, as if purposely positioned for maximum visibility. A tall figure in outsized sunglasses, scarlet lipstick, and a huge fuchsia pink silk head scarf unfolded herself on to the pavement, floral skirt swinging beneath a mink jacket.

"The speed limit's twenty through this village," said Hector tersely, as the driver stretched her arms and legs, wobbling on high heels.

Tommy, running back along the pavement at full pelt, stared as Hector put a strong hand on the visitor's shoulders. He drew her towards the door of his flat, stopping only to fish his house key out from under a pot of snowdrops and turn it in the lock before they disappeared up the stairs together.

"The speed limit signs are there for a reason, you know," we heard him say as he pushed the woman firmly across the threshold. "You need to kill that throttle, if you know what's good for you."

Tommy took a step back as he pulled out his diary and started scribbling in it. I read over his shoulder what he was writing: "Hector Munro said he wanted to throttle Mrs Minty."

I was about to explain that throttle meant something different in this context, then thought better of it for fear of getting into a conversation about Minty's true identity. Plus it would be rude to admit to reading over his shoulder.

Tommy closed his diary, stuffed it back in his pocket, and turned to look at me wide-eyed.

"So what do we do now?"

I considered my words carefully to protect Hector's secret. Perhaps this was the real Minty, and Hector had simply been her editor. If not, allowing someone else to be mistaken for Minty could provide a useful decoy.

I cleared my throat. "As Hector seems to have a meeting, I'd better get back to tending the shop."

Tommy frowned. "Then I'll carry on working on this case by myself." And with that he stumped off in the direction of the village shop.

I tried to concentrate on bookshop business till closing time, although my heart was pounding. Who was the stranger anyway? For a moment I even wondered if it was Celeste. Perhaps Celeste was Minty, or the books had been a joint venture between her and Hector, and she'd come to claim her share of the takings. I'd always imagined Celeste to be shorter and slimmer.

Maybe it was Celeste who Horace had accompanied on the flight, not some random billionaire. Or maybe Celeste was a billionaire now, having made her fortune in Australia. Women can be billionaires too.

As long as she hadn't returned in hope of a reconciliation, I might just about cope with meeting her.

I took comfort from the fact that Hector's greeting had hardly been friendly. Normally so gentle and tender, he'd given the stranger a forceful shove into his flat. By now they might be having a fight. Or she might be holding him hostage. She looked robust enough to overpower him. Notwithstanding her high heels, if it came to a fight, my money would be on Miss Minty.

I suddenly felt like I didn't know Hector at all.

Annoyingly, a steady trickle of customers began to appear from nowhere, as many as we'd normally have on a busy Saturday. Most were middle-aged women with a strangely furtive look about them. They lingered, browsing, for ages, and those who ordered tea or coffee made their drinks last until they were cold.

When Ella, who never visited the shop on a weekday, came charging purposefully through the door at a quarter to five, I beckoned her behind the counter.

"What's going on?" I asked in a low voice. "Suddenly half the village is here, just when Hector's decided to take the afternoon off, too."

"Has he taken Hermione Minty to The Bluebird? I didn't think it opened till six. Mind you, Donald's wife's a big Minty fan, so I'm sure he'd be prepared to open up especially for her."

125

"What do you know about Hermione Minty being here?" I couldn't believe how fast word spread in the village.

"One of the mums told me when she picked her kids up from after-school club. She heard it from Carol, who got it from Mrs Crowe, who said Dinah had told her you were planning to fix up a visit from Hermione Minty. Honestly, Sophie, you might have given me a bit of notice that she was coming today. I'd like to have brought my mum to meet her."

The mention of her mother was like a bolt of lightning to my brain. The car was Nancy's, but the driver was far too tall to be her. Of course! Hermione was Horace in disguise.

So this was his idea of a publicity stunt to help us sell more of her books. I closed my eyes, trying to picture the scene upstairs, and wished I had a baby monitor to hear their conversation.

Ella rapped on the counter to regain my attention. "So where are you hiding her? In the stockroom?"

I chewed my lower lip. I couldn't get away with fibbing to Ella. She knew me too well. I kept my voice to a whisper.

"Actually, she's upstairs with Hector."

Ella's eyes widened. "And are you happy about leaving your boyfriend alone with a steamy romantic novelist?"

I grinned. "I'm quietly confident that Hermione Minty holds no temptations of that nature for Hector."

"So when are you going to bring her down? That's what all these people are hovering about for. Didn't you realise? They're hoping to get a glimpse of her."

Certainly half of them were currently holding Minty books.

I thought quickly. "Not today. I think she and Hector are talking terms. I hear Miss Minty's a shrewd businesswoman. She'll probably name an appearance fee so vast that we won't be able to afford it, and that will be the end of the matter."

Ella narrowed her eyes. "But think how much business you'd get out of it. The woman has rarity value. Mrs Crowe told me Minty never makes public appearances. This would be a real coup for Hector's House. You'd be mad to turn her down, whatever her price."

I shrugged. "I agree, but what can I do? It's Hector's House, not mine."

She frowned. "Well, tell him from me, I think he's a fool if he doesn't sign her up." She glanced at her watch. "But now I must dash. I've got a governors' meeting to prepare for tonight. I'll catch up with you soon."

She headed for the door, and then turned to call over her shoulder to me. "Don't forget, if you do book Hermione Minty, give me as much notice as possible so I can bring my mum."

As soon as I'd shut the shop — I'd had to turn off the lights to persuade the last few stragglers to leave — I slunk round to the side of the building, squeezing past the green Mini. Retrieving Hector's front door key from beneath the pot of snowdrops, I unlocked the door to his flat as quietly as I could, replaced the key in its hiding place, and tiptoed up the stairs.

Hector and Horace were sitting opposite each other in the fireside chairs, like a pair of disgruntled bookends. Both were leaning forward and talking tersely. Horace had ditched the shades as well as the headscarf. The only light in the room came from the wood burner, blazing away in the dusk. They'd clearly been too intent upon their discussion to even notice that it had got dark while they'd been talking. Nor did they acknowledge my arrival.

I coughed. Neither looked round. I flicked on the ceiling light, which made them both blink and go quiet. Then Hector turned to glare at me, while Horace, mock cheer in his voice, said, "Hiya, Sophie. I thought I'd take your advice and come to see my big brother when I was sure to find him at home."

I perched awkwardly on the coffee table, rather than the sofa, diplomatically equidistant from each brother. Trying to lighten the mood, I pointed to my lips.

"Horace, I don't think film star scarlet is your colour. Bright lipstick is so last year. This spring's going to be all about the natural look. You'd be better with a nude."

"Sophie Sayers, you little flirt!" said Horace, spluttering with laughter, but Hector was not amused. Blushing as I realised what I'd said, I clapped my hands over my mouth.

"At this point, I'm not sure I want your opinion," said Hector, unsmiling.

I frowned at him. "You don't think this stunt was my idea, do you? It's all down to Horace."

Horace shot me an apologetic look. "That's right. It was my idea. I thought it would be good for business."

"And to be fair, he was right," I said quickly. "The shop's been heaving since Horace arrived."

Horace brightened. "See? I told you it was a good idea. What do you want me to do next? I've got time on my hands till I go back to Oz. I'm not leaving now till the fifteenth of Feb. The airline is practically paying me to fly with them then."

Hector looked at him sternly. "The best thing you can do is get downstairs, ditch those fake plates, and get going, before word spreads any further that the village's favourite author is at large."

Horace scowled. "Those fake plates cost me fifty quid. I'm not going to chuck them in the bin."

"If you leave them on and the police stop you on your way home, you'll be charged for fraud. You could even end up getting Mum's car confiscated."

I gasped. "Really? Just for the sake of a practical joke?"

Hector nodded while Horace shook his head. They looked like Tweedledum and Tweedledee but with a healthier BMI.

Horace sighed. "Oh, for goodness sake, Hecate, lighten up. Don't you get it? I'm on your side. Can't a brother help a brother now and again?"

For a few awkward moments, neither said anything, then Hector stood up, pulled his Swiss Army knife out of the pocket of his jeans, and flourished it towards Horace. I wondered whether anyone had ever used a Swiss Army knife to commit murder, and if so, which of the blades would be the most effective murder weapon.

"I'm going down to remove those plates now, and then you're taking Mum's car back," he said. "You did ask her whether you could borrow it first, I presume?"

Horace pouted. "Maybe."

Hector headed for the stairs. Once he was safely out of earshot, I took his fireside chair.

"Horace, I'm sorry if I got you into trouble."

Horace patted my knee. "It's not your fault, sweetheart. We make our own luck in this life, and we make our own trouble. I am guilty as charged. But don't worry, he'll get over it."

Easy for you to say, I thought, as I watched Horace pad gently down the stairs barefooted, leaving the floral skirt, headscarf and jacket in a pool on the floor, like the residue of the melted Wicked Witch of the West. His vacated high-heeled shoes stood neatly beside his still-warm armchair. I wondered whether Nancy had missed them.

15 Dead Writers' Society

"So who told Horace about Minty?" When Horace had departed, Hector's tone remained cold. "I made Mum promise me ages ago that she'd never tell anyone, not even my dad, so she definitely won't have told Horace. I have only ever told you, Mum and May."

And Celeste, I added in my head, but I didn't want to remind him of her existence. He was gazing at me intently as if expecting me to confess.

I hesitated. "Maybe it's a twin thing? Perhaps when he was reading one of your mum's Minty books, like you said he did, he recognised the pattern of the language, as if it was his own words? I mean, twins have that sort of bond, don't they? Finishing each other's sentences and that sort of thing?"

For a moment, I almost convinced myself that it wasn't my fault.

Hector shook his head. "I don't think so, Sophie. I don't write the books in my own voice. I write them as a vibrant young woman. Hardly Horace's voice either, I think you'll agree."

I allowed myself a small smile. Perhaps Hector wasn't going to blame me after all. Perhaps he realised the prospect of Horace knowing his secret identity wasn't as big a problem as he'd thought.

Auntie May used to say to me, "Nothing is as good as you think it's going to be, and nothing is as bad as you think it's going to be." When she first said it, I thought she was being a killjoy, but the older I got, the more I appreciated her philosophy.

My relief was short lived. "I don't need Tommy's detective skills to work out that the number of suspects is reduced to one," said Hector, "what with May Sayers being no longer with us."

To set the record straight, I thought I had better confess.

"OK." I held my hands up in mock surrender. "It's a fair cop. I didn't let the cat out of the bag, but I sort of led the horse to water. And he drank."

Hector frowned. "Ignoring that rather mangled set of metaphors for a minute, I can't believe you are telling me you actively told Horace about my pseudonym. You, of all people, Sophie. I really trusted you."

"No, no, that's not how it was at all, honestly. I just happened to have a copy of *Angel Heart* lying about in my front room, and he picked it up and by chance opened it at a page where a woman is described who he says looks exactly like Celeste. Then he saw your dedication to her." I paused to allow Hector time to apologise for not having removed his loving tribute to his ex, but he said nothing. "That was enough to make the penny drop."

Hector paled.

"And when was Horace in your front room exactly? I thought the afternoon of, er, Hermione's surprise appearance was the first time he'd been in the village since you moved here."

I clapped my hand over my mouth at my indiscretion. "He – he called round last Monday while you were at the library meeting. He said he just wanted to check me out."

Hector's eyes blazed. "He did what? How dare he? The first girl I've been serious about for years, and he has to muscle in!"

He strode across the room, turned his back to me, and stood staring out of the shop window, arms folded tightly across his chest.

I wasn't going to stand for that kind of language.

"Muscle in? As if I'm some sort of inanimate brainless trophy for idiotic men to squabble over. Next you'll be telling me that you're going to challenge him to a duel with pistols at dawn, or play poker, with me as the prize."

I was trying hard not to get distracted by the fact that he'd said I was the first girl he'd been serious about for years. It had started to feel as if there were three people in this relationship: Hector, Horace, and me. No, four with the ghost of Celeste still hovering, and five with Hermione lurking in the background, taking notes of our dilemma for use in her next novel.

Then Hector spun round and shot me a black look. "I need some air." He glanced at the clock on the wall. "I'm going out. Can I leave you to lock the door behind you when you leave, Sophie? Can I at least trust you to do that?"

He didn't pause long enough to notice that I wasn't going to dignify his unworthy jibe with an answer. Snatching up his jacket, he added, "All my life, I've been glad that Horace was spared when he was so ill, but now I think the sooner he's despatched, the better."

"Despatching him? That's a little harsh, isn't it?"

I tried to make a joke of it, as if he meant fratricide, rather than just wishing his brother back in Australia.

133

Hector wasn't listening. Car keys jangling in his hand, he headed for the door. "As for Hermione Minty, I think you've just made up my mind for me. I'm going to kill her off. I've had enough of her. Good riddance to the wretched woman."

In the silence that fell after he'd stomped down the stairs and slammed the door behind him, a wave of relief rushed through me. I felt as if he'd just ended an illicit affair. I hoped it wasn't the end of us, too.

I peered out of the front window, watching Hector drive into the distance in his Land Rover. Tommy, skulking by the wheelie bins lined up on the kerb for the morning collection, stared after him for a moment, then started writing something in his diary.

Next day, Hector still hadn't returned, so, feeling slightly sick, I opened the shop and ran it on my own all day, trying to look as if nothing was amiss.

Towards the end of the afternoon, as I was washing up the tearoom dishes, Tommy sauntered into the shop. Diary still in hand, he watched my every movement closely, as if he was a public health inspector. I gave Billy's jug, distinctively labelled *The Grapes of Wrath* from our Literally Gifted range, so that we always knew which one was his, an extra polish with a tea towel, before topping it up ready for the morning with an inch or two of hooch from the brown glass bottle that lived in the fridge.

"I've had cough mixture in a bottle like that before," said Tommy conversationally. "Is that medicine?"

I looked up to find his gaze fixed on the hooch.

"No, of course not, Tommy. It's just a particular brand of cream that Billy likes in his tea and coffee."

I took it over to the sink and topped it up with filtered water from the jug in the fridge.

"Then why are you putting water in it? What's that do?"

"It waters it down."

Tommy narrowed his cat-like eyes. "Really? That doesn't look like water in that fancy jug thing. Are you sure it's not some sort of a catapult?" He leaned forward over the counter and lowered his voice. "Does it turn it into poison?"

Puzzled, I returned the bottle to the fridge. Then I realised what he meant. "Did you by any chance have a chemistry lesson at school today, Tommy? I think you mean catalyst, not catapult."

He gasped. "How did you know?"

"Anyway, why on earth would I want to poison Billy?"

"He might be blackmailing you. Or perhaps you're a serial killer and this is your mode – your moody—"

"*Modus operandi.* Honestly, Tommy, do I look like a serial killer?"

He narrowed his eyes again while considering this. "You might be a master of disguise. Or covering for Hector."

I cursed the day I'd recommended the junior detective book to Sina for Tommy's Christmas present.

"Covering what for Hector?"

"His guilt, of course."

"And what might his crime be, exactly?"

"I don't know. I'm still working on that one."

And with that, he left the shop.

Just when I felt like hiding in my cottage and locking myself in for the night, I was obliged to go back to Hector's House after tea and open it up again for the next meeting of the Wendlebury Writers.

135

When I returned to the shop, I was strangely relieved to see Hector's Land Rover was still missing from its parking space, though I kept an ear open for the sound of its return throughout the meeting. I wasn't sure whether or not I wanted Hector to do his usual trick of leaning out of the flat's window as I locked up after the meeting to call me in for a late-night drink and a chat. Seeing him again so soon might compound rather than resolve our dispute.

Most of the meeting passed me by in a blur, as the members discussed, topically, the many forms of romantic writing, and whether and how they chose to tackle it themselves. I only really tuned in when Dinah admitted that she was having a stab at a romantic novel herself, as she finally felt in the right place in her life. Knowing looks and indulgent smiles ricocheted around the table. We were all pleased that her latest romance, first evidenced back at the village show in the summer, was still going strong.

I gazed at Hector's empty stool behind the counter, wondering whether Dinah's romance would outlive my own.

"So is she going to honour us with a visit or not, Sophie?" said Dinah.

I jumped. "Who? Your girlfriend? You should know. I'm sure she can if she likes. She seems very pleasant."

Dinah tutted. "Please try and keep up, Sophie. We're talking about Hermione Minty."

"Oh, yes, of course, Hermione Minty. I mean, no, sorry, I'm afraid she can't visit us at all."

"What, not soon, or not ever?" Julia asked.

"Yes, can you be more specific, please?" Dinah's pen was poised over the minutes book.

"Not ever, I'm afraid. The thing is, Hector told me that she's dead."

There was a sharp intake of breath all around the table. Jacky was first to speak.

"Hermione Minty dead? Surely there must be some mistake. There's been nothing in the papers to suggest she'd been unwell."

"Nor on social media, either," said Karen. "She seemed hale and hearty enough on her Twitter account last time I looked." She pulled her phone out of her bag and swiped to her Twitter app. "Mind you, she's been a bit quiet for a couple of days. Even so, that's rather sudden."

I tried to look sad. I didn't need to try very hard. "Maybe she'd scheduled those tweets ahead of time. Or she might have been ill for longer than it seems, and has an assistant keeping her Twitter timeline full, as a smokescreen to allow her to spend her declining days in peace."

"What a brave lady," sighed Jessica. "Always putting her readers first."

Considering Hermione had only joined Twitter a couple of weeks ago, that was a generous tribute.

"Or her bottom line," said Jacky, the shrewdest businesswoman in our group, as she ran her own commercial dental practice.

"What do you mean?" asked Bella.

Jacky waved her hand dismissively. "Don't you realise sudden death is a great boost for an author's profile? Existing fans will start rereading her books to catch up on any they've missed, while new readers will be drawn to them out of curiosity, lured by headlines and obituaries, to see what all the fuss is about."

Dinah sniffed. "All the same, dying suddenly is not something even the most money-motivated author would do on purpose."

Jessica perked up. "Perhaps she knew she was ill and wanted to depart at the height of her powers, so as to maximise the benefit for her literary heirs."

"Did she have many children?" asked Julia.

"A couple of daughters, I think," said Jessica thoughtfully. "Both grown-up, of course."

I had no idea where that came from.

Dinah pointed to the shelf of my Auntie May's books. "I remember May Sayers' books sold out here the day after her death, and Hector had to restock twice before her funeral."

"They still sell very well even now," I said. "You'd think everyone in Wendlebury would have her complete works by now, but we still get people coming in every week to buy various books as gifts for friends and relations. Her commentary on the Cotswold Way is a favourite with tourists and walkers passing through."

"Still, it's unfortunate timing for us, just when we'd started building such a good relationship with Hermione Minty," said Dinah, tapping her minute book to bring us back to the agenda. "I heard she'd even had a meeting here with Hector just yesterday to plan her visit."

"Oh Sophie, what was she like?"

"Did you get to meet her?"

"Lucky you!"

I chose my words carefully. "To be honest, I only saw her very briefly in passing. The meeting took place in Hector's flat, for the sake of privacy." All of this was true. Well, sort of. "But I did think she looked a bit peaky. I wasn't entirely surprised when Hector told me the bad news."

"I wonder why she never mentioned her ill-health on her website?" said Jacky.

"She was a very private person," I said, confidently. "She didn't like people to know her whereabouts, never mind her state of health."

Dinah sighed and crossed "Plan Minty visit" off her agenda. "Oh well, it can't be helped. We're lucky we got her endorsement for our Christmas book while she was still *compos mentis*."

"Now she's dead, it'll probably sell well next Christmas too," said Jacky brightly. "And her new novel is bound to be a runaway bestseller. I heard it's due out in a couple of weeks, though I can't remember its title. Sophie, can you please order me a copy tomorrow when the shop opens?"

"And me, please."

"Two for me."

"Me too."

I fetched the order book, jotted down their names, and left it on the counter ready to action when we opened up next day. I thought it would lighten Hector's mood when he came back in.

If he came back in.

16 The Mint Unwrapped

"Mum cried when I told her about Hermione Minty being dead," said Tommy next afternoon after he'd come home from school. "She said it was a shame she wouldn't be able to write any more books."

"That seems a reasonable conclusion, Tommy," I said, pouring myself a cup of tea. "Though my friends at the Writers' group last night were saying she'll probably sell more now that she's died."

"That will make Hector happy. He really likes selling books, doesn't he?"

I nodded. Tommy was silent, which was generally more cause for alarm than Tommy being noisy. I could see that he was thinking hard and building up to some wild statement.

"So if books sell more after authors die, I suppose that makes it tempting for people who run bookshops to murder authors? Because then they'll make more money?"

I nearly choked on my tea. "I don't think so, Tommy. Booksellers are by and large law-abiding."

"But Hector was telling me the other week that some of the best authors are dead."

"He was talking about the authors of classics – people who were writing over a hundred years ago. They're bound to be dead by now. All authors have to die eventually."

Tommy looked around the shelves as if scanning for clues. He pulled out a book at random.

"What about this one?" He held up a copy of *Great Expectations*.

"Well, yes, obviously Charles Dickens is dead."

He crossed the room to the fantasy section and picked up a Terry Pratchett.

"Sadly, yes, he's dead too, though he died far too young."

Tommy held the books side by side to compare the author photos on the back. "They look pretty similar to me."

He stuffed both books into a space on the dictionaries shelf and wandered over to the travel section. He held up May Sayers' Cotswolds guide.

"She was your auntie, wasn't she? Do you sell a lot of her books?"

I nodded.

"And she's dead."

I could hardly disagree. He gave me an 'I told you so' look.

"It's put me right off writing books when I grow up," he said. "It sounds far too dangerous."

At that point, Hector, looking slightly sheepish, entered the shop for the first time in two days. He didn't look me in the eye, or even say hello but glanced around as if checking that everything was in order.

"What's dangerous?" he said to Tommy, clearly glad to have an ice-breaker that excluded direct contact with me.

"Being an author," said Tommy. "All these dead authors. I mean, look at them. It's like the shop's a graveyard." He looked around and shuddered. "OK, I'm out of here. See you later, miss. See you, Hector."

After Tommy's departure, Hector turned to me, still smiling, though I could see he was forcing it a bit.

"I – I'm sorry about dashing off like that the other night, Sophie." He swallowed hard. "I went down to Clevedon to sort things out with Horace. I thought I ought to make the effort to see a bit more of him while he's at home. To be honest, it was a bit awkward at first, after our row."

I bet it was.

"But Mum made me realise that Horace's intentions were of the best, and by the time she'd convinced me, it was too late to drive home, so I stayed over. Then she made us go out for a pint last night to make things up, which turned into more than one, so I ended up staying another night at Mum and Dad's. It was just like old times, sharing a bedroom with my brother." He chuckled a little self-consciously. Then he put his hand to his temple. "Still feeling a bit groggy, to be honest. But I'm sorry, I should have texted you rather than take it for granted that you'd keep the shop running for me without being asked. I knew I could depend on you, though."

I wasn't sure how to take this. "So all's well between you and Horace now? Are you friends again?"

He cleared his throat and marched round to take up his usual seat at the trade counter. "Me and Horace, we're a team," he said quietly. "Always a team."

I suppressed a smile. "Of course."

He clearly wanted to draw a line under the whole thing. It was a relief to know Horace had put his mind at rest, which meant mine could be at rest too. I now believed that Horace's intentions in visiting me truly had been to prevent his brother from being hurt.

Hector stretched his arms in preparation for a typing session, then looked up from his computer for a moment.

"By the way, what was Tommy on about? Which famous author has died now? I haven't seen the news today."

I hesitated. "Er, Hermione Minty."

"Hermione Minty? Hermione Minty's dead? What on earth do you mean? How can she be? Who killed her?"

I gulped. "You did. You said you were going to kill her off."

I hated to revive our harsh exchange, but he seemed to have forgotten.

Hector leapt up from his stool. "What? But she's my cash cow. My goldmine. My golden goose who lays my golden eggs."

I backed away behind the display table.

"Now who's mangling their metaphors? You said she was more trouble than she was worth."

Hector covered his face with his hands. "Surely you knew that was just in the heat of the moment? Of course I'm not going to kill Hermione Minty. I'd be a fool to do that."

Feeling a little unsteady, I leaned on the display table and stared down at it in silence.

"So have you told everyone she's dead?" he asked. "I thought you were meant to be the great marketing expert?" He had never used such a bitterly sarcastic tone towards me before.

I raised my hands as if in surrender. "I never claimed to be an expert. You just told me I was. And you told everyone else, too. It's embarrassing. Donald has been expecting me to work miracles to bring in extra punters to his pub, because of what you've said to him about my supposed magical marketing powers."

But Hector wasn't listening. "If you wanted to be smart about it, you could have simply made Hermione Minty go missing, like Agatha Christie did back in the day, when her marriage broke up. Don't you know about that? She ran away to a hotel in Harrogate and lay low there while she came to terms with the shock of her failed relationship. When the press got hold of it, she hit the headlines of the nationals. Something like that would have given a healthy boost to our sales. Or you could have sent her off on a fictitious round-the-world cruise. But no. Now she's dead, she's nothing but a back catalogue."

"But you're not dead, Hector. You can always write more books under a different name. Maybe you'd like to write books in a different genre for a change. One that comes more naturally to you."

"What, like *Confessions of a Bookseller*? In case you hadn't spotted it on our shelves, that's already been done. Anyway, it's taken me years to establish Minty's reputation. Some people will buy any new book that comes out simply because her name's on the cover. There's no point throwing that kind of loyalty away and starting all over again from scratch."

"I'm afraid you're going to have to. Unless, like Dr Who, she can regenerate, it's too late."

"Actually, it might not be too late. Same thing happened to Mark Twain," said Hector tersely, turning away from me. "He had to put out a statement saying 'Reports of my death have been greatly exaggerated.' It seems Hermione Minty is in good company."

"Hector Munro, I am arresting you on suspicion of the murder of Hermione Minty. You do not have to say

145

anything—" here Tommy pulled out his diary to read the rest of the statement that he'd written down earlier "—but anything you say may later be used in evidence."

Having reached the end of his script, he marched over to the trade counter and grabbed Hector by the wrist. I half expected him to produce a pair of handcuffs from the bottomless depths of his Parka pockets. Instead, he stopped and looked around, as if expecting reinforcements to come to his aid. The shop door swung open, and a couple of passers-by, sensing some unusual activity, came in to join the small crowd staring at the scene from the other side of the display table.

Bemused, Hector let his wrist go limp in Tommy's grasp. "So what now, Officer Crowe?"

Tommy's face clouded for a minute. "I was rather hoping you'd give me a lift to Slate Green Police Station so I could turn you in." He dropped Hector's wrist. "Feel free to get your car keys, whenever you're ready," he added pleasantly.

There must have been a chapter in his detective skills book prescribing the classic nice cop, nasty cop routine.

Hector clasped his hands on the counter top.

"And on whose authority are you acting, may I ask?"

The nasty cop resurfaced. "The law of the land. It's against the law to murder people, and I'm allowed to arrest other people if I see them breaking the law. It's called a citizen's arrest. It says so in my book."

I determined to take the remaining copy of Tommy's detective handbook off our shelves and return it to the publisher for a refund.

"The law of the land also says I'm innocent until proven guilty. Or didn't your book mention that little detail?"

"Yes, but I've got proof. Hang on."

146

Tommy slipped his bulging backpack off his shoulder and on to the counter, immediately drawing out two regulation vehicle registration plates, one white, one yellow, and holding them up for everyone to see.

"I found Hermione Minty's personalised number plates in your dustbin after she disappeared without trace on the day of her visit to you." He looked down at his diary again. "During the afternoon of the twenty-fifth of January, I observed her going in to your flat at sixteen fifteen hundred hours and she never came out again. Then later, her car mysteriously disappeared while I was having my tea. Its distinctive number plates turned up after dark in your wheelie bin, when it was left out for collection."

I wondered whether Tommy made a habit of raiding wheelie bins, or whether that honour lay solely with Hector's.

Hector, looking impressed, put a finger thoughtfully to his lips. "So what do you deduce happened to the rest of the car, once I'd taken off the licence plates and thrown them away?"

Tommy scribbled this down under the heading 'Confession'. "I'm still working on that," he said quickly. "But in the meantime, I must ask you to accompany me to the station where my colleagues in uniform will take your statement."

I admired his faith in the system.

"Couldn't you just bring Bob down to the shop?" I asked, thinking that the presence of our resident policeman would cut this nonsense short.

Tommy turned to me. "I did call for him, miss, but he told me to go away because he was busy watching *Countdown* on telly."

Well, Bob was off duty.

Suddenly conscious of his audience of a dozen customers in the shop, plus a growing crowd outside on the pavement looking in through the window, Tommy reached again for Hector's wrist. Hector, too quick for him, stood up and stuffed his hands into the pockets of his jeans.

"What about Hermione Minty's body? Have you found that yet?" Hector seemed to be enjoying himself now, obviously wondering how far he could stretch Tommy's powers of invention. I could imagine him and Horace playing games of cops and robbers when they were little boys.

"It'll almost certainly be in the car when I find it," said Tommy. "Unless you've buried her in your garden. Or you might have dumped her in a disused quarry, or cooked and eaten her."

Tommy's mum must have been letting him watch films unsuitable for his age for him to have had that idea – or perhaps the television news.

Then Tommy turned to me.

"I'm sorry for the inconvenience, miss, but I expect you'll be allowed to visit Hector in prison."

Hector frowned. "What about my trial? The British justice system isn't like a board game, Tommy. You can't just give me a 'Go directly to jail' card."

The shop door jangled open.

"What, you mean you want to pass 'Go' first? That's cheating. You have to go to prison."

"Who's going to prison?" asked a familiar woman's voice behind me.

"Hector, for the murder of Hermione Minty."

Neither Tommy nor I took our eyes off Hector, and Hector was staring, challengingly now, at Tommy.

"How absurd," came the reply from the familiar voice. "Hermione Minty is alive and well and living in Clevedon."

"Really?" I said, as all three of us swivelled round in surprise.

"Yes, and I can vouch for her safety. You see—" the elderly lady drew herself up to her full height, a couple of inches shorter than Tommy "—I am Hermione Minty."

A collective gasp went round the shop, and a loud squeak came from the direction of the window, which had multiple noses pressed against it for a better view of the action.

"No, you're not, you're Hector's mum," said a middle-aged lady by the cookery books. "Hello, Mrs Munro, how are you? Good to see you back in Wendlebury. We missed you at last year's Village Show."

Nancy turned to her with a smile. "Hello, my dear. Yes, we were sorry not to make it, but I had to go to my old school reunion in Dorset that day. I hope you're still enjoying that Edwardian side table I sold you?"

"Fits in my front room alcove a treat," said the woman warmly.

Tommy coughed loudly. "Excuse me, we've got serious business to attend to here. How can you be Hermione Minty?"

"It's my pen-name, Tommy. My, you've grown a lot taller since I last saw you. How is your mother getting on? And little Sina? Do give them my love."

"They're fine, thank you, Mrs Munro. But if you're Hermione Minty, I'm going to have to see some proof."

Nancy glanced across to the display table with its usual pile of Minty books, but before she could pick one up, Tommy had a brainwave.

149

"If you're Hermione Minty, where's her car? It's a racing green Mini with a National Trust sticker on the windscreen and a knitted purple blanket folded on the back seat."

"You mean that car?" She pointed to the road outside the shop where her Mini was parked neatly at the kerb. "If you need any further proof, I can tell you the plot of every Hermione Minty book on that table."

"I could do that too, but it doesn't make me Hermione Minty," called a woman in the crowd who I recognised as a regular buyer of Minty's books. "It doesn't mean I wrote them."

Nancy let slip an ever so slightly smug smile. "Ah, but could you tell me the plot of her next book? I can. And you won't have to wait long to check whether my evidence is correct, as it'll be published next month."

Tommy narrowed his eyes. "So you're not dead, then?"

Nancy looked down at herself as if for evidence. "No, I'm not dead yet."

"So Hector didn't murder you?"

"My Hector wouldn't do a thing like that."

Tommy's shoulders sagged as he turned back to Hector, who had slumped down on his stool behind the trade counter, looking bewildered. "I suppose you're free to go, then. I'll let you off with a caution for now." He reached for the number plates and held them up to Nancy. "But what about these? You can't drive your car without number plates."

For a moment, I thought he might console himself by arresting Nancy for a motoring offence.

Nancy cast a disparaging look at the discarded plates. "They're only decorative, Tommy. Hector's brother's idea of a novelty gift. You can only put personalised

150

licence plates on a car if you've bought the right to use them from the DVLA."

"So they're not really any use to you?"

"No, that's why I took them off Mum's car," said Hector, pulling himself together now. "To prevent her from committing an offence."

"When Horace bought them, he meant well, of course," added Nancy. "So I don't think he should be punished, do you?" This was directed as much to Hector as to Tommy. I wondered how often she'd had to stop them coming to blows when they were little boys, before Horace became too ill to squabble.

"Good intentions or not, I've no need for them now," said Hector briskly. "Having them around would irritate me. That's why I threw them away."

Tommy perked up, but before he could purloin them, I had a better idea.

"Why don't we give them to Donald, to help him promote The Bluebird's Minty-themed Valentine's Dinner? He could even add them to the raffle hamper as a novelty prize."

"So if I buy a raffle ticket, I might get to keep them?" Tommy was easily consoled.

I didn't like dampening his enthusiasm, but didn't want him to be disappointed. "Provided you buy the winning ticket."

But Tommy was ever the optimist. "I'll take them over to the pub now, if you like, to get them out of your way." Bemused, Hector nodded assent. "Thanks, Hector. See you around."

And with that, he was gone, shop door banging behind him. For a moment, we relished the silence.

"So that's my reputation restored as a law-abiding citizen," said Hector with a lopsided smile. "I don't think

I was ever in real danger there, but thanks anyway, Mum." He came out from behind the counter to kiss her on the cheek. "What are you doing here, by the way?"

She gave him a hug, then unbuttoned her coat and made for the tearoom. "Carol invited me to meet her daughter, so I've just had lunch with them both. What a pleasant, bright young girl that Becky is, with extraordinary inner strength to have survived her difficult childhood. She and Carol seem to be getting on famously, and the baby's adorable. Shame there's no father in the frame, but no matter. Though it must feel like poetic justice to poor Carol."

She draped her coat over the back of a chair and settled herself down at a table, her large handbag on the floor beside her.

"I can't help worrying there's a catch, but as you know, I do like a happy ending. Don't let me hold you up, dears." She pointed at the queue of people clutching Minty books at the trade counter. "I'll make myself a cup of tea and you can join me when your customers have all gone."

As Hector turned the "Open" sign to "Closed" on the shop door and started to cash up, I went to join Nancy with a fresh pot of tea. Not wanting to miss this opportunity for a one-to-one chat, I leaned my elbows on the table, ready to grill her.

I couldn't wait to ask her the burning question of the moment. "So are you really Hermione Minty?" I said in a low voice.

Nancy laughed. "Not really, dear. I only said it on a whim. When I heard that boy accuse my Hector of murder, I couldn't help myself but jump in and protect him, even though I knew it wouldn't be possible to murder a character who he had invented. Well, unless you're Sir Arthur Conan Doyle, bumping Sherlock Holmes off at the Reichenbach Falls because he'd had enough of him. It would be like assassinating his imaginary friend." She paused to drink some tea from a Nancy Mitford cup. "Still, it's not a complete fib. I could claim to be the inspiration behind her. You see, I suggested to Hector a few years ago that he might do a bit of writing to earn some extra cash when he needed it, and thus Hermione Minty came into being."

I was grateful for her tact. "It's OK, I know all about Celeste, and their circumstances – that he had to support her while she was ill. It must have been very difficult for him."

A shadow passed briefly across her face. "He'd been talking about supplementing the income from his day job with evening bar work. I didn't think that would be good for him, so I came up with the writing idea as something he'd actively enjoy. He'd always been a good little writer when he was at school."

"What sort of stories did he write when he was a boy, Nancy?"

"When Horace was ill in bed for so long, Hector used to entertain him with stories written especially for him. He invented a dynamic duo. Their *alter egos* were indestructible superheroes who would go round saving the world together. Obviously it was wish-fulfilment, not only pretending Horace was healthy, but investing him with superpowers. Everyone who heard them remarked on the quality of Hector's writing. I always hoped he might take it up again eventually."

"How sweet! What did he call the dynamic duo?"

Nancy smiled indulgently at the memory. "Horatio and Hecate. He picked the names out of an ancient companion to Shakespeare that we had in the shop, thinking they sounded like secret-code versions of their actual names. They still use them now and again as a term of affection, an admission of their past vulnerability and how they overcame it together. They can overcome anything if they stand together. People can, you know."

"I thought it was only Horace who was ill?"

"Oh yes, but Hector felt it too. Don't mistake their choice to live on opposite sides of the globe as a lack of closeness. They're still in each other's pockets, wherever they are in the world."

"I did wonder what they were on about when I heard them use those names at your house that Sunday," I said. "But wasn't Hecate one of the three witches? And therefore a woman?"

"I'm glad you know your Shakespeare. Unfortunately the boys didn't realise that until years later when they were studying *Macbeth* at secondary school. I could have told them, of course, but when Hector showed me the first story he'd made up, all beautifully written out in his best handwriting, I didn't have the heart to tell him. Besides, people do strange things with names these days, don't they? Isn't there a woman writer who has James as her first name? Or is it Nigel? What were her parents thinking?"

I smiled. Though the names of her children had struck me as unusual at first, I loved them both now.

"Horace still teases Hector about his error. Hector's comeback is that Hecate was originally the name of a goddess, rather than the mere mortal prince that Horatio was."

"Still, it must have been quite a jump from comic-book action to romantic novels."

"Yes, and I had to help him make the transition. I suggested some nice romantic plots to start him off. I've always read a lot of romance, so I knew exactly the sort of thing that readers like. I thought it would be good therapy for him, too – escapism from the stress of his daily life. Not his day job, I don't mean." So she was no fan of Celeste's either. "The poor boy had got so thin with worry."

She leaned towards me, dropping her voice to almost a whisper.

"I was incensed when Hector dedicated his first book to that woman. I could see the relationship would never last, and she didn't deserve it. But of course, I couldn't say so, because it might have driven him further into her clutches. I was very glad to see the back of her when she chose to leave, even though it did break his heart for a little while."

I didn't want to dwell on the subject. "So is Hector effectively your ghost writer?" If Nancy was providing the plots and Hector the words, that's what it sounded like to me.

Nancy shook her head. "Only for those first few stories. I just fed him some happy endings." Her eyes widened innocently.

"To show him what a good relationship could be like?" I was impressed by her cunning.

She leaned in again. "Yes, but I'm not sure he ever realised what I was up to. Please don't tell him."

I decided to read *Angel Heart* after all. I might pick up some good advice.

"Now he writes them all entirely on his own, but he always shows me his finished drafts before publication. He has a professional editor and proofreader, of course, but I'm touched that he still values my opinion." A smile played about her lips. "You'll like the next one. I think it's his best yet."

"I'll look forward to reading it," I said politely, hoping I'd like it as much as she did. "Speaking of ill-fated relationships, did Carol confide in you about a certain someone threatening to return to the village?"

Her smile vanished, making me wish I hadn't brought the subject up. "Yes, and I'm very worried on her behalf. I don't know how that wretched man can show his face here. The few people who remember the fiasco with Bertie will not welcome his return. Or else they'll welcome him back with pitchforks and scythes."

I hoped she was joking.

17 Booked Up

After all the upheaval of the last few days, I wasn't sure Hector would want to go to Donald's Minty-themed Valentine's Dinner with me. But Nancy's supposed confession lifted his mood considerably, especially when she pointed out the financial advantages of being able to wheel her out for book signings and talks in other shops and literary events, providing useful publicity for Hermione Minty's books while still keeping her real identity a secret.

As for Nancy, she seemed to be relishing the idea. Within days of her revelation, she had committed to speaking at three Women's Institute groups and four bookshops.

Word quickly got round the village, and in the February issue of the parish magazine, alongside my column about narcissi and Narcissus, Wendlebury Barrow Village Show Committee announced that Hermione Minty would be guest of honour at the next annual show.

Next time we went down to Clevedon for Sunday dinner, Horace seemed to think the pleasing outcome had all been down to his intervention, and Hector had the grace to let him get away with it.

It was heartening, though still odd, to see the pair of them together. Hector even persuaded Horace to accompany us to a car boot sale, on condition that we joined him at The Moon and Sixpence afterwards.

Consequently, we didn't make it back to Wendlebury till the next morning, driving up at the crack of dawn to open the shop on time. But it was worth the hangover to feel that I'd bonded a bit with Horace, and that Hector and he were once more the best of friends.

In truth, despite the fact that Horace's impulsive nature had almost spelled the end of my romance with Hector – not to mention the sudden death of Hermione Minty – it was hard to say goodbye to him on 13 February, when he came up to spend a final evening in Wendlebury before he was due to head to Heathrow the following evening, ready to catch his flight in the early hours of the fifteenth.

Meanwhile, bookings had been going well for The Bluebird's Valentine's Dinner, with every table reserved in advance. Donald had also sold hundreds of raffle tickets at a pound a time, a huge boost to his takings for the new year.

On Valentine's Day, I left Hector's House a little earlier than usual to go to help Donald set up. Hector had promised to join me at 7pm for the meal. Ella met me at The Bluebird, and together we laid out the tables in a fancier way than for the usual pub grub menu.

What a difference our extra touches made to the ambience. The addition of a tiny potted pink primrose on each table for two, donated, along with a discount voucher, by the Slate Green Garden Centre, really lifted the mood of the room. I was astonished how generous the centre manager had been. We had more than enough for every table, plus one for each place setting at the big round table that Donald had set aside for singletons, at Ella's thoughtful suggestion. Even after we'd put a few primroses on the bar, there were some spares.

"Have one each to take home, as a little thank-you for all your hard work, girls," said Donald.

"Don't you want to keep them to put in your window boxes?" I asked, not wanting to take advantage.

"They're already full of herbs, Sophie. If I had my beer garden finished now, I could put them out there, but that's going to take a couple of months, and the flowers will have faded by then. Go on, you have them."

We added a tall, tapering red candle to every pot for an extra romantic touch. Carol had dug out from her trunk of old material a spool of machine-made lace, which she'd allowed us to cut into strips to make small runners for the centre of every table. While Donald wasn't looking, Ella made a circuit of the pub, sprinkling on to the upholstery oils of rose, lavender and sandalwood that she'd brought from home. She swore by aromatherapy as the key to jumpstarting a romantic evening. As the central heating kicked in before opening hours, creating a heady atmosphere, I hoped she hadn't overdone it.

Once we'd laid out all the cutlery and glasses on the tables, Ella and I perched on bar stools for the welcome cup of coffee that Donald had brewed for us, while his wife was hard at work in the kitchen, preparing fifty covers of the set meal.

"Ella, I never asked who your date is," I said, poring over the checklist of table bookings that Donald had left on the bar. "Are you still seeing that fitness instructor from the leisure centre?"

Ella grinned. "I'm doing much more than seeing him."

I noticed her table was in a discreet corner of the bar, and I made a mental note to check him out at least from a distance when they arrived.

"I see Kate's down here too, with her husband," I said. "That's nice. In fact, I know most of the names here."

My heart sank when I saw Ted's name 'plus one'. I was happy for him that he'd found someone else to bring, but disappointed on Carol's behalf.

"You'll probably know all of the faces too. And speaking of faces, I'm going to go and put mine on while it's quiet. There's still half an hour before anyone's due to arrive."

She grabbed her make-up bag and hairbrush from her handbag.

"I'll whip home and slip into something more comfortable," I called after her as she headed to the Ladies'. I'd meant to bring a smart dress to work that morning, but had forgotten. "See you shortly."

As I passed the village shop, Carol caught my eye and beckoned me inside. I glanced at my watch, not wanting to be delayed. Chats with Carol were never quick.

"You're open late tonight, aren't you? You're usually closed by 6pm."

She wrinkled her nose. "Well, I didn't think it was worth going home before I go to The Bluebird. I just wanted to say I'll see you later. Becky's told me I've got to go up to the pub to present the raffle prize. She said Donald thought it would be a nice way to thank me for donating the chocolates and the lace. I suppose it's a good way of reminding everybody to support the village shop. Every little helps."

She took off her customary full-length apron to reveal a flattering midnight blue jersey dress underneath, far smarter than she'd usually wear to work.

"Gosh, that's pretty. That colour really suits you. Are you sure you're only going to present the prize?" I winked at her, hoping that she had a date after all.

Her face fell. "Sophie, I cannot tell a lie. I'm afraid I've agreed to meet Bertie there. Just once, just quickly, and then I'm going to tell him that there's no way we can get back together. We were barely ever together at all, apart from, you know, Becky…"

"Does Becky know you're meeting him?"

"Goodness, no," she said quickly. "Please don't tell her. It had got to the point where I thought that if I didn't meet him face-to-face, he'd never stop pestering me. And perhaps I owe him that much."

I sighed. "To be honest, Carol, I don't think you owe him anything at all. But if this will allow you to draw a line under the whole relationship and move on, then it's not my place to discourage you."

It was unfortunate that her timing was so bad, just as dear Ted had hooked up with someone else. Goodness only knew how long it would take her to find another suitable beau. Perhaps she never would.

"Where are you meeting him? Surely not for dinner at a romantic table for two?"

She shook her head. "No, I'll have cheese on toast when I get home. But first I'm meeting him in secret, out the back, in the courtyard, beside the well. You may think that sounds silly, but that's where we used to do our courting. In those days, you could still smoke in pubs, so hardly anyone went out there in the winter. It was a good private place to meet, with dark corners and shady sheds to hide in. Quite romantic in its own way." She sighed wistfully. "Though I confess, I shan't be sad to see it all bulldozed and replaced by Donald's new beer garden."

"I'm not sure there's room for a bulldozer in there. I can't see how they'd get one round the back. But I do know he's getting the well filled in with concrete tomorrow. Ella and I were having fun lobbing old bits of rubbish down it just now. I can quite see why Tommy's so fond of it."

"Yes, bless him."

"Apparently, Donald's going to keep the little wall around the well in place, but put a false bottom in there above the concrete filling, with a bit of water in it, so that it still looks like a traditional well. I bet children in the play area will be pestering their parents to throw coins down it."

"Another extra income stream for the pub, then." I had to admire her business acumen, usually so well hidden. She'd done a remarkable job keeping the village shop afloat in these days of online ordering and deep-discounted grocery superstores.

"Thank you for your support, Sophie," said Carol, reaching across the counter to take my hands. "I think this is all for the best."

As she let go, I caught sight of my watch. "I'm sorry, Carol, I must fly. I've just got time to dash home and change before I've got to be back at the pub to help Donald dish out the welcoming Mint Juleps. You'll know where to find me if you need me."

"Yes. Enjoy your special evening, Sophie. You've worked hard for this. I hope you and Hector get your just desserts."

Used to her creative use of English, I took that as a compliment, not a threat.

"Mint-flavoured, of course," I replied.

Opening the wardrobe, I couldn't decide which of May's extensive collection of exotic dresses to wear. She'd brought so many back from her trips abroad during her travel-writing days. It was the sartorial equivalent of a luxury box of chocolates, with so many textures, colours, and weights, all sumptuous and rich.

Eventually I pulled out a slender sheath dress of dark brown velveteen, lined with the palest ivory silk, a sliver of which peeped above the scooped neckline. Only as I was dashing out the door did I realise I had subconsciously chosen a frock that made me look like an After Eight.

I grabbed my handbag, almost knocking over Donald's primrose, perky and lush against the crumbly black potting compost. As I was about to leave, the front door of Joshua's cottage creaked open. A rustling of plastic suggested he was putting rubbish in his wheelie bin. I felt awful leaving him to spend Valentine's Night alone with his memories of his late wife, and of my Auntie May, his childhood sweetheart and companion after his wife died. I grabbed the primrose and swung my front door open quickly to catch him before he had time to get back inside.

"Happy Valentine's Day, Joshua," I called cheerfully, reaching across with the pot plant in my hand. "This is for you."

His face lit up. "And a very Happy Saint Valentine's Day to you too, my dear." He took the flower pot and held it up to my security light to see it better.

"Pink to make the boys wink, eh, my dear? How kind of you to think of me. I must give you something in return."

Thoughtfully, he appraised my dress, visible under my still unbuttoned coat, and set down the primrose on top of his wheelie bin. One hand to his aching back, he stooped down to the wooden tub of spring bulbs by his doorstep and broke off a single snowdrop at the base of its stalk. After hauling himself back upright, he reached across the hedge to slip the slender green stem into my hair, the tiny flowers resting above my right ear. When he tenderly touched my cheek, I realised what a loss he must have been to Auntie May, and she to him, when she left him in her youth to travel the world.

18 The Silent Tree Falls

Having run all the way to the pub so as not to be late after my exchange with Joshua, I made straight for the Ladies' to touch up my make-up before taking my place to greet diners on arrival with a tray of Mint Juleps. As I passed the side door, I heard a funny noise outside, from the direction of the courtyard. I opened the door and stepped outside to investigate, the frosty flagstones squeaking beneath my feet. It didn't sound like Carol.

"Who's there? Surely no-one's smoking out here on Valentine's Night?"

Wary of interfering with Carol's clandestine meeting, yet also concerned for her safety - and for the smooth running of Donald's Valentine's Dinner - I tiptoed into the shadows. As I entered the unlit courtyard, a rustling noise was coming from the back of a tumbledown shed due for demolition.

"Billy, is that you?" It looked a bit like him. I took a few steps forward. "Billy?" I said it louder now, to make sure he could hear me.

The figure stepped forward slightly, and Billy's eyes peered up at me from under a battered cloth cap.

"I ain't that little sod," came a gravelly reply. "And don't you go telling him I'm here, neither."

Daring myself to take a step closer, I realised it wasn't Billy but Bertie. Though there was a strong family resemblance, he was a shadow of his younger brother's stocky self. Billy was still able to wield a scythe and dig graves in the churchyard. Bertie looked as if he'd have trouble lifting a pint of beer, though he certainly smelled like one.

"Nor no-one else, neither. There's only one person I want to see here tonight, and it ain't you, May Sayers."

I feigned ignorance.

"I can't tell anyone you're here because I don't know who you are."

He grumbled to himself for a moment, picking up a discarded cigarette end from the ground.

"You don't need to tell no-one nothing in any case. It's none of your business."

If Carol was entertaining even the slightest idea of giving him a second chance, the sour smell wafting across from his unwashed body would surely repel her. I wondered whether I could change his mind about staying in the village and get rid of him before she arrived.

"If you need a place to stay tonight, try calling at the vicarage. The vicar's got connections with the local hostel down in Slate Green."

"I don't need no bloody vicar. And if I wants to get to Slate Green, I knows the way, thank you very much."

"But you've missed the last bus. And you can't stay here. These sheds are going to be demolished in the morning, when the lorry comes to fill the old well with concrete."

He took a step towards me.

"What do you take me for? I've got no intention of spending the night in some old shed. As soon as I've attended to my business of the evening, I'll be moving into somewhere a lot warmer. So you keep your beak out of it, missus."

I hoped that warmer place would not be Carol's fireside, or, perish the thought, her bed.

Hearing voices in the street as guests for the Valentine's Dinner approached the pub, I remembered my duties and scurried back inside.

Returning to the fragrant warmth of The Bluebird was as comforting as stepping into a hot bubble bath, not least because of Ella's earlier generosity with the essential oils. Even though I'd had no physical contact with Bertie, I felt soiled by my encounter, so went to dart back into the Ladies' to wash my hands and spritz on a little perfume.

The Ladies' was now occupied, so after a quick look round to make sure there weren't any men approaching, I darted into the Gents' opposite. Both were single cubicle rooms, the mirror image of each other, so it wasn't as if I was invading anyone's privacy, although subsequent visitors might wonder why the Gents' was smelling of Auntie May's Chanel.

To disperse the evidence of my perfume, I stood on the toilet seat to release the catch of the small high window. As a gust of icy air blew in, I thought I heard a splash, and for a moment I assumed my mobile phone had fallen down the loo again. But the splash had come from a different direction, from beyond the open window, and my phone was safe in my handbag, beside Auntie May's travel-sized perfume atomiser.

The splash had come from the courtyard. Perhaps while I hijacked the Gents', one of the male diners had

167

been caught short, forced to wee in the well out of desperation. He'd better not do that after the courtyard got its new look.

Impatient to return to the bar without further distractions, I threw open the toilet door energetically, almost knocking Billy off his feet as he loitered by the side door, presumably heading to the courtyard for his habitual smoke. He was the last person I expected to find at a Valentine's Dinner.

"What are you doing here?" I asked, nervous of him bumping into Bertie. When he looked blank, I said it again, louder.

"Ah!" he said, catching it this time. He tapped behind his ear to indicate he'd forgotten his hearing aids. Then he pointed at the Gents' sign. "I might say the same to you."

Before I could reply, the latch lifted on the courtyard door, and Carol came in at high speed, bumping into both of us.

"I didn't expect to see you here tonight, Bill," she said pleasantly. "Don't you know it's Valentine's Day?"

"I don't care what day it is, but I do know it's like Piccadilly Circus in here tonight. Can't a fellow have a quiet drink without being harassed?" He stepped back to appraise Carol's dress. "Well, you're a sight for sore eyes, missus."

Carol giggled nervously. "Becky said I scrub up well."

Billy's gaze lingered. "Yes, you always did," he said, quietly by his standards. Then he coughed. "Anyway, I'm glad I seen you because I've got a message for you. That baker chap is in the pub somewhere looking for you. I expect he'll be glad of the opportunity to eat someone else's cooking rather than his own bloody awful cakes." He pointed across to a table where Ted was sitting by himself, surreptitiously popping a breath mint into his mouth. "Now, if you ladies will stop accosting me, I'm going through to the public bar for a pint. There's none of this lovey-dovey nonsense going on in there."

We stood back, allowing Billy to pass. Carol leaned closer to me.

"I'll let you into a secret, Sophie. Billy used to be a little sweet on me when I was younger. My mum told me after I'd returned to the village that Billy said if his brother ever crossed his path again, he'd duff him up. Sibling revelry, eh? It makes me glad to be an only child."

She looked across at Ted and took a deep breath. "My goodness, Sophie, I do believe Becky has set me up!" I wished I'd thought of doing that. Ted caught her eye and broke into a broad smile, before getting up to draw out the chair opposite, beckoning for her to come and join him. "It looks like someone else is expecting me. I suppose I'd better go and say hello."

I bit my lip. "I think it's more than a hello that he's after, Carol."

She lingered for a moment, as if struggling to digest her good fortune. I grinned. "Gosh, you've been bemoaning the lack of men for ages, and now you've got three of them fighting over you! But what happened with Bertie? Have you seen him yet?"

She held up her hands. "Would you believe it? It looks as if after all that fuss, Bertie's threats and promises have come to naught. I've just come in through the courtyard, and he was nowhere to be seen. It was all nothing but talk. Unreliable as ever. Still, I'm not complaining. When one door closes, another one locks."

Giggling, she gave Ted a coquettish wave.

"Do you know, when Becky told me to dress up posh, I had no idea what she was up to. I'd make a terrible detective, wouldn't I, Sophie?"

19 The Girl with Forget-Me-Not Eyes

As soon as I had finished dishing out the Mint Juleps and returned the empty tray to the bar, Donald said I was free to join Hector, leaving the teenagers he'd hired as waitresses for the night to serve the food.

"All the guests are here now, apart from a couple of no-shows on the singles' table," said Donald.

Arriving at our table, I was pleased to see Hector had ordered a bottle of champagne but hadn't yet touched a drop. The only other couple to have an ice bucket on a stand beside their table was the vicar and his wife. Although I suspected Donald had only two ice buckets, that made me feel special.

The Reverend Murray cut a dashing figure in a cream silk cravat and burgundy shirt. If I hadn't known he was a vicar, I would never have guessed. Opposite him, Mrs Murray's stiff gold cocktail dress reminded me of the foil on chocolate coins. She must have been glad to wrestle her husband away from his pastoral duties, even if they were surrounded by his parishioners.

As I sat down opposite Hector, he filled our glasses, and we raised them to each other in a toast.

"Happy Valentine's Day," we said, simultaneously. Then Hector added, "Everything OK, Sophie?"

I must have seemed distracted, because the little scene with Bertie was still running through my head. Supposing Billy discovered him while he was having a cigarette? I hoped Donald's special romantic evening wouldn't be spoiled by a bar-room brawl, nor Carol's evening, nor Ted's.

From time to time, I glanced nervously at the side door, yet all seemed still out there. It was quiet in the public bar, too, without the usual noisy banter ping-ponging around. Jukebox music had been supplanted by a classical CD featuring a delicate string quartet. Even the jangling of the fruit machine had been silenced in the interests of the ambience.

I gave a little shiver of satisfaction at the part I'd played in bringing this whole evening together. It was giving so much happiness and satisfaction to so many people – to Donald as publican, to Carol and Ted, to the Reverend and Mrs Murray, to Kate and her husband, to Ella and her fitness instructor, and all the other happy couples seated ready to enjoy an intimate evening together. Not least, to me and Hector.

Tonight was no time to be thinking of family feuds. Tonight was the night for love and reconciliation, for healing old wounds and generating new memories. It would soon be spring, a time to look forward to new beginnings, not stir up old quarrels.

I glanced across at Ted and Carol, in time to see him tentatively reach his hands, so strong and muscular from all that kneading, across the tablecloth. She moved hers closer to allow him to clasp them. I hoped this new romance might bring Carol the happy ending she'd craved for so long, and which she so richly deserved.

A clatter from the side door heralded the arrival of Tommy.

"What were you doing out there?" asked Hector as Tommy passed our table. "Taking the scenic route home?"

"I wanted one last look at the well before it gets filled in. I just chucked my last ever things down there for old times' sake."

"Can someone your age have old times?" asked Hector wryly.

"That well's been there all my life, and tomorrow it'll be gone. That's a big thing for me, Hector."

"It won't be entirely gone, Tommy, just changed. It'll still look the same from the outside."

"Same difference," said Tommy briskly. "I feel a bit sad."

I squeezed Hector's hand as a warning not to tease Tommy any further. The boy had had enough loss in his young life, and if it helped him to say goodbye to the well in his own way, that was harmless enough.

Donald called over from behind the bar, where he was busy uncorking wine bottles.

"Have you got a date, Tom?" He winked at me conspiratorially. "I didn't see your name on the list of bookings. Does your mum know you're here? Because you shouldn't be, not unless you're with an adult eating a meal. It's against the law. I'm sorry, son, but I'll have to ask you to leave, or I'll get into trouble."

Tommy wandered listlessly over to the bar.

"I hope you don't want me to arrest myself. I've only come in to see whether I've won the raffle."

Donald put down his corkscrew. "Look, I've told you once, Tommy, I can't sell you a raffle ticket, because the

173

prize contains alcohol. You'll have the law after me if I do."

Tommy pulled a tiny scrap of rose-pink paper out of his pocket and held it up to show Donald. "You don't have to sell me one. I've got one already."

Donald took the ticket from him to scrutinise. "It's definitely one of my tickets. But how did you get hold of it? I've only been selling them to customers in the pub."

He returned the ticket to Tommy, who held on to it with both hands.

"Billy gave it to me. I did him a favour, and he gave it to me as my reward."

Donald considered for a moment. "OK, we'll do the draw in a minute, then you must go home."

He produced a small plastic tub of folded raffle tickets from under the counter, then raised the flap on the bar to step out into the room. Tommy settled down to watch the proceedings from a bar stool while Donald marched over to Carol and Ted's table and offered her the plastic tub.

"Carol, as one of the generous donors of the raffle prizes, will you please do the honours and draw the winning ticket?"

With a little squeal of excitement, Carol let go of Ted's hand. Closing her eyes so that she couldn't be accused of choosing a particular ticket, she stuffed her hand deep into the tub and pulled one out from the very bottom. She smiled, opened her eyes, and passed the ticket triumphantly to Donald, who unfolded it, hesitated for a moment, glanced around the room at the expectant faces, then read the number aloud.

"Three hundred and seventy-two."

A rumble went around the room as everyone commented on however close their own number was to the winner. Then Tommy sprang from the bar stool and waved his ticket aloft.

"That's me, that's me, that's me!"

Everyone cheered.

Donald's face was the picture of surprise. "Really, Tommy, are you sure? Let's see your ticket again."

Solemnly, Tommy held it out to him, Donald taking an age to reread the little black figures.

"Yep, you've won fair and square," he said at last. "Well done, lad."

Everybody clapped and cheered again, either genuinely pleased at the boy's excitement, or not wanting to look like sore losers in front of their dates. Tommy made to seize the prize hamper from where it was displayed at the end of the bar, but Donald put a restraining hand on his arm.

"I can't let you take it away without your mum present." He indicated the bottle of pink champagne. "But if you give your mum a ring, she can come and collect it now."

Tommy frowned. "She can't. She's at home with Sina. She can't leave Sina on her own. It's against the law."

Funny how well acquainted he was with the laws that suited him. He shot an anxious look at the hamper, as if worried someone might snatch it from him.

"OK, then tell her to bring Sina with her. Look—" Donald pointed to the singles table "—we've had a couple of no-shows, so why not ask your mum if all three of you can stay and eat dinner with us, as an extra bit of prize? My wife always overcaters, so we've plenty to go round. It'll only go to waste otherwise."

Touched by Donald's kind gesture, I resolved to eat in The Bluebird more often in future, as a show of support. Auntie May would have called it karma.

175

Then the waitresses started to bring out the first course, colourful melon balls steeped in Crème de Menthe, and everyone returned their attention to their dates.

"Hector, did you see that?" I leaned forward to speak confidentially. "I think Donald just rigged the raffle. He made Tommy win. He memorised the number when Tommy showed him his ticket the first time. When Carol gave him the winning ticket, I think he only pretended to read it. Did you notice how quickly he folded it up and put it back in the tub before anybody could check it? It could have been anyone's ticket."

Hector grinned. "Of course he rigged it. Didn't you see him and Carol wink at each other? They were about as subtle as a pair of pantomime villains. Why do you think Carol didn't read the number off the ticket herself, but handed it straight back to Donald?"

I laughed. "Like a game of wink-wink murder, only the prize was the hamper instead of death! Do you think anyone else guessed?"

"If so, they didn't seem to mind. Though I bet Billy will when he finds out, as he bought the ticket. Still, it's not like winning the Lottery. And it'll teach Billy to take advantage of Tommy."

"Whatever favour it was that he did to earn Billy's ticket, I'm sure Tommy will think he got a good deal."

I grinned. Billy was always getting Tommy to do his dirty work for him.

But Hector wanted to move on.

"Speaking of rewards, Sophie, I've got a little surprise for you, too." He fixed me warily with his green eyes. For one moment, I feared he might be about to propose. I glanced into my champagne glass to check he hadn't concealed an engagement ring in it.

He reached under the table and pulled out a flat rectangular package neatly wrapped in turquoise tissue paper. He pushed it across the table to me, slaloming around our brimming glasses. Just a book, then. Relief coursed through me, as well as slight disappointment at his lack of imagination. After all, he was constantly giving me books he thought I ought to read. It was starting to get a bit annoying.

"Thank you," I said quickly. I didn't want to hurt his feelings by seeming ungrateful.

Slowly I untied the ribbon and peeled back the little gold seal that was holding the edges of the tissue paper together. I'd had the parcel upside down, so the first thing I saw was the back cover. I recognised the familiar pastel illustrations in the style that appeared upon every Minty novel, but I hadn't seen this one before. In all the mayhem, I'd forgotten her latest book was due out the following day.

I flipped it the right way up and discovered the best Valentine's present ever: *The Girl with Forget-Me-Not Eyes.*

"You've got the wrong colour eyes for Virginia Woolf," Hector had said to me at the village show back in the summer. "Hers were grey. Yours are forget-me-not blue."

"Go on, open it," he said now, gently touching my hand. "There's a personal inscription inside.

I smiled at Hermione's extravagant signature on the dedication page. Nancy's imitation of Hector's original was excellent.

"To my number one fan," he'd added, with a giant kiss. But what meant far more was the dedication above, printed by Hector in every copy, for all the world to see: "For Sophie, with all my love".

I reached across the table to take both Hector's hands in mine.

"I love you too," I said. Then we sat for a long time saying nothing, our fingers intertwined, with the champagne bubbles rising and rising, unsipped, to burst at the top of our glasses.

20 February Sale

The crowd outside Hector's House next day was so large that the pavement couldn't contain it. A police car was parked on the road outside, and two policemen, arms outstretched, were trying to keep the crowd on the pavement, safe from passing cars, horses and tractors.

My heart began to race as I put two and two together. Had someone been murdered? Perhaps someone was about to be arrested, and a mob had gathered to watch. I started to run, desperate to know Hector was safe, but Bob had already spotted me.

"Late for work, Sophie?" he called out cheerfully.

I forced a smile. "Not quite. But what on earth are all these people doing here? What's going on? Have you come to arrest someone?"

I looked about for "Crime Scene – Do Not Enter" tape, but found none.

Bob grinned. "Funnily enough, I'm here to buy a book. My sergeant sent me down to get a signed copy of the new Hermione Minty book as a belated Valentine's present for his wife. Apparently, he's in the doghouse for working late last night. When he saw on the local breakfast news this morning that Hermione Minty would be launching her new book in Wendlebury, he thought that would be just the thing to make it up to her."

I put my hands over my mouth in shock. "Hermione Minty's going to be signing books here today?"

A lady in the crowd leaned over to me. "Did you think she was dead too? I know, we all did for a bit, but apparently it was just a rumour."

A woman I recognised from behind the counter at Slate Green Library backed her up. "That's Twitter for you. Always saying people are dead when they're not."

As they stepped back into line, not wanting to lose their place in the queue, I turned back to Bob in hope of a further explanation.

"When me and my mate got here and saw the crush," he said, "we thought we'd kill time waiting for Hector to open up by practising our crowd control techniques. We don't often get the chance to control crowds round here. I don't think we've ever had a riot, not even in Slate Green. Still, I suppose you'll be wanting to get into work."

To create a passage through to the front door for me, he edged across the pavement, arms stretched out in front of the crowds, and his colleague did the same opposite.

"Go on through, love, and get Hector to save me a book for my sarge, will you?"

I took a deep breath, and strode assertively to the door, which was still locked. Tommy, unaccountably already inside the shop, released the catch just long enough for me to slip inside. As soon as I'd entered, he slammed the door shut, put the chain back on, and headed for the stock room.

"If they've all come to bring you Valentine's cards, they're a day late," said Hector cheerfully from behind an improvised signing table in the far corner of the shop. He was just setting up a cardboard sign saying in big letters "MEET HERMIONE MINTY".

"Who are all those people?" I asked, slipping my coat off and hanging it on its usual hook. "Half of them aren't even from the village."

"Seems like they've rumbled that I was launching Hermione Minty's new book here this morning. A Hector's House exclusive, no less! Now they all want a piece of her. Apparently it's been all over social media this morning, with pictures of the shopfront and maps of how to get here. Goodness knows how they found out."

We turned to peer at the crowds through the shop window. Many were clutching dog-eared copies of old Minty books, presumably eager to have them autographed. Others had purses at the ready to buy her latest.

"You won't make much money if they've brought books with them," I said.

Hector raised his eyebrows and pointed to the central display table. Since I'd left the shop last night, he'd completely restocked it. Instead of the usual array of books by different authors, it was now entirely covered in copies of *The Girl with Forget-Me-Not Eyes*.

"None of them will have this one yet. You got the first copy last night, remember? I'd kept the rest of the consignment hidden in the stockroom so as not to spoil your surprise. I had enough printed to last till the summer, but looking at the crowds outside, I'm not so sure. So, I have to eat my words and thank you, Sophie, for putting the word out on Twitter. You were right, I was wrong, and I have to say I'm very glad of it."

"But how did it get onto Twitter last night, Hector? I haven't tweeted for days."

At that point, Tommy emerged from the stockroom, trailing a long strip of bubble wrap, idly popping bubbles as he walked.

"And what are you doing here, Tommy? Why aren't you at school?"

"It's half term, miss. Surely you knew that?" I did, but in all the excitement, I'd forgotten. "I've been in the shop helping Hector this morning, stamping on the cardboard boxes as he unpacked them. The boxes he'd been emptying Mrs Minty's books out of. And I've been helping him with the new window display, too."

"But the shop's not even open yet."

"After all the fuss on Facebook last night, I thought you'd be having a busy morning, so I came round after breakfast to see if Hector wanted any extra help. He's giving me a free copy of this new book for my mum if I keep it a secret."

"What fuss on Facebook? What secret?"

"I'll grab the last box of books," said Hector, disappearing into the stockroom. "I think we're going to need them."

Tommy was looking so pleased with himself that I thought he might burst. "Hermione Minty's secret identity. I told you I'd discover untold secrets about the village. And I did. Hermione Minty isn't Hector's mum at all. Didn't you know?" He paused for dramatic effect. "It's Hector." He hugged himself with excitement. "Can you believe it? Hector is Hermione Minty. He asked me not to tell anyone, but I don't think you count."

I decided to interpret that as a compliment.

"You will keep it a secret, won't you, Tommy? Please? It's important."

Tommy gazed at me incredulously. "Of course I will, miss. Hector's my friend. And his mum is a nice lady.

Hector said his mum likes pretending she's Hermione Minty, and he didn't want to upset her. I can understand that. I don't like upsetting my mum, either."

"And you mustn't tell your mum about this."

Tommy nodded. "It's ok, I didn't. But Hector did say I was allowed to tell her that he would be selling signed copies of Hermione Minty's new book here today, and that he'd give me a signed copy for my mum. Besides, my mum read about it on her Facebook fan club page last night."

"There's a Minty fan club on Facebook?" My new online publicity campaign for Hermione Minty hadn't got as far as Facebook yet.

Pulling my phone from my bag, I logged into Facebook and typed Minty's name into the search box, which led me to a group page called 'Hermione Minty Fan Club', bearing the enigmatic profile photo copied from her Twitter account and a collage of her book covers. Posts about today's book launch at Hector's House had been commented on and shared by numerous enthusiastic readers.

Hermione Minty's Facebook following, like the queue outside the shop, was growing by the minute. But who on earth had set up the Facebook account, if not me or Hector?

Then, in my head, I heard Twitter's little blue bird laughing at me like a gleeful kookaburra. Clicking instinctively on 'page info', I found the name of the group's administrator: Horatio Oz.

Swiping to Minty's Twitter account, I discovered @HoratioOz had been busy there too, posting with the hashtag #HermioneMintyBookLaunch.

Horace may have told me he had no time for social media while negotiating the dangers of the bush, but I remembered he had Twitter and Facebook addresses on his koala-shaped business card. He must have understood their power for publicity. How better to while away the wait for a long-haul flight at Heathrow than by giving his twin brother a helping hand online?

I turned back to Tommy, one more mystery left to solve. "How did you find out Hermione Minty's true identity?" I asked Tommy, genuinely intrigued.

"When I came into the shop before it closed last night to buy a Valentine's card for my mum, I saw Hector signing that book about flowers for you. I thought it was funny that he was signing it 'Hermione'." He stood up straight, shoulders back, like a policeman reporting for duty. "I caught him red-handed and made him spill the beans. He squealed, he confessed, he sang like a canary." Hector must have been lending Tommy his DVDs of old black-and-white detective films. "And I didn't even need to take his fingerprints."

"Good work, Tommy."

He shrugged. "Anyway, Hector said I deserved a reward for solving the mystery, so he gave me this book."

He held up a copy of a book that I recognised from our post-Christmas sale stock: *101 Things for Boys To Do.*

"Now I've got 101 new hobbies, I'm not sure I'll have time for any more detective work. I hope you're not disappointed, miss."

When Hector came out from the stockroom, he had Nancy in tow. He leaned forward to whisper in my ear. "I forgot to tell you that I'd invited her to come up this morning. Horace and I thought it would take her mind off him flying back to Oz today."

I was glad I'd left his flat after breakfast to go home to change before she had arrived.

Nancy stopped to kiss me warmly on the cheek, before settling down at the signing table.

I smiled at her. "Cup of tea, Mrs Minty?"

She beamed. "Ooh, I'd kill for a cup of tea!"

Tommy checked his Parka pocket for his diary, realised it wasn't there, and sighed in defeat.

Hector followed me to the tearoom to get a glass of water for the signing table.

"I can't believe you told Tommy the truth about Hermione Minty," I hissed. "What on earth made you give in so easily after all these years of secrecy?"

Hector shrugged. "I can hardly believe it myself. That boy has a disarming directness sometimes. I guess he just caught me off guard. But don't worry, I've sworn him to secrecy. Despite all his faults, he's an honest enough lad."

We looked across at Tommy, standing by the door, hopping excitedly from one foot to the other.

"It's nine o'clock, Hector, shall I open up for you?" he called across to us, before unlocking the door without waiting for an answer.

The crowd spilled in like water from a burst main, pooling around Nancy and grabbing copies of *The Girl with Forget-Me-Not Eyes* as though they were on ration.

Glancing around the tearoom to check all was well, I spotted on one of the tables a sheet of paper on which Hector had clearly been training Nancy to emulate Hermione's autograph. I grabbed it, screwed it into a ball, and stuffed it in the pocket of my jeans, planning to stick it on the fire when I got home so as to destroy the evidence.

"Why didn't you tell us Hermione Minty was coming?" Julia called to me from the signing queue.

185

"We're jolly lucky to catch her," said a stranger, sparing me from answering. "She doesn't usually do public appearances."

"Last time I saw Hermione Minty was at Cheltenham Literature Festival three years ago," said another.

"No, you're thinking of Katie Fforde," said her friend. "It was at the Hawkesbury Upton Lit Fest that we saw Hermione Minty. She was awfully good."

"Of course, she's changed her hairstyle since then." The pair of them gazed at Nancy approvingly. When she smiled back and gave them a little wave, they giggled like infatuated schoolgirls. I wondered who it was that they'd seen at Hawkesbury, as clearly it couldn't have been Nancy, but I decided not to correct them. I didn't want to put a damper on their excitement.

The only customer to bypass the signing table was Billy.

"I've just come from The Bluebird," he said, elbowing his way through the crowd.

"Crikey, that's a bit early even for you, isn't it, Billy? Breakfast at the pub?" I hoped my trick of watering down the tearoom's cream hadn't made him resort to an alcoholic breakfast.

"I never said I went inside, girlie. I only passed by, and before you so rudely interrupted, I was about to tell my young friend here that the concrete lorry's just arrived." He turned to Tommy. "If you want to go and watch them pour the concrete down the well, you'd better get down there quick, or you'll miss all the action."

"Ooh, I'm off, then! I want to make a handprint before it dries."

"Like film stars do in Hollywood?" I asked.

"Like my cat did on next door's patio."

As Tommy scampered off to make his mark, I headed to the tearoom counter, bracing myself for an onslaught of customers, once the crowds had scored their signed copies. They'd need liquid refreshment to restore themselves after all the excitement. As I set out cups and saucers on the counter, Bob and his colleague approached, their boss's book tucked under Bob's arm.

"Got any takeaway cups, please, Sophie?" asked Bob.

"Sure," I smiled. "I think you deserve a drink on the house after your masterful crowd control out there."

Bob grinned. "No cream for us, though, thanks. Not while we're on duty."

His colleague looked puzzled but said nothing. I was relieved to know that the law was happy to turn a blind eye to Hector's little hobby. Or at least, Bob was.

I raised the glass dome from a plate of jam tarts. "Go on, have one for the road," I said. Perhaps that wasn't the smartest phrase to use in the circumstances.

As they left the shop, Billy got up from his favourite table, where he'd been waiting patiently for me to serve him. He slipped off his jacket and left it over the back of the chair to save his place. He'd clearly had an egg for his breakfast again, or most of an egg, anyway. I was confident that his jacket would keep people away from his table.

I wondered why he was approaching the counter to place his order rather than bellowing it across the room, as usual. When he started fiddling with his hearing aid, I realised that all the background noise might prevent him from making out what I was saying unless he was close enough to lipread.

To my surprise, he leaned towards me over the counter and began to speak in a very low voice.

187

"Sophie, love." I couldn't remember him ever using my name before, never mind any terms of endearment. For the sake of hygiene, I moved the plate of cakes from in front of him to the other side of the counter.

"Yes," I said tentatively, assuming he'd come out without his wallet and was after a freebie. There was no way I was going to start a tab for him.

"I gather you had the misfortune to meet my big brother last night."

I nodded, unsure what he wanted me to say.

He forced a laugh, as if trying to make light of the matter.

"So it was you, then. I thought it must have been, going by his description. Do you know, the silly old fool thought you were your old auntie. He told me how well he thought May Sayers had aged. Ha! She were twice your age last time he set eyes on her, and that were more than twenty years ago."

I struggled to check his mental arithmetic but quickly gave up.

"Of course, he was just playing for time telling me that before we got down to business. But he won't be making that mistake again. I think he's gone for good after what I had to say to him last night. He won't be bothering Carol any more, and he certainly won't be bothering your old auntie, God rest her soul. He's destined for the other place."

"What, Slate Green?" I asked, pleased to think he might have taken my advice about the hostel, rather than trying to cadge a bed with Carol or Billy.

"I honestly can't tell you where he is now, girlie." Back to his usual manners, then. "But I've no doubt he won't be seen no more about the village, not after the home truths I told him." He sighed. "I don't know how he could think I'd take his side after what he did to Carol, even if I am his brother."

He fell silent, perhaps remembering happier times when they were carefree boys in the village together, doing no greater mischief than the kind Tommy Crowe got up to now.

"You sit down, Billy," I said gently. "I'll bring your tea over. And some cream."

After the upset he'd been through the night before, today the cream would count as medicinal.

Just as I'd set his order on the table, there was a loud crash at the door as Tommy burst in with even more than his usual energy. His eyes were bright, his cheeks flushed, and he was so puffed out from running that he could barely speak.

Barging past browsing customers, he took the unprecedented step of coming round behind the tearoom counter to join me. Seizing a tumbler from the draining board and filling it with water from the tap, he downed it in one, refilled it, and only then paused to explain himself.

"Are you ok, Tommy?"

"I'm ok. I'm fine." He lowered his voice. Why did everyone have to speak in whispers today? "But the dead body down the well isn't."

He paused and stared at me, wide-eyed.

"What?" I hissed. "Really? This isn't another one of your games, is it, Tommy? Not like the business with Hector and Hermione Minty?"

He scowled. "That was no game, miss. And nor is this. There's a real live dead body down the well at The Bluebird. I've just seen it. I thought it was Billy at first, because it did look at a bit like him, but I know it can't be him now because he's here."

My heart was pounding so fast that it was hard to keep my voice to a confidential whisper. "Does Donald know about it?"

"He does now," said Tommy. "I've just told him. He sent me back here to see if Bob was still here."

"You've just missed him. Run back and tell Donald to dial 999. But first, how did you discover it?"

Tommy straightened his back proudly. "It was me. When I got there, the concrete men hadn't started. They were still messing about talking to Donald out the front, so I thought I'd take the opportunity to have one last go at throwing things down the well while they weren't looking. Donald had tidied everything up so there wasn't much to chuck. All I could find was a dirty old shoe. Just the one shoe." He raised his hands in disbelief. "I mean, who leaves a single shoe behind without noticing? Honestly, my mum complains about me losing stuff at school, but at least I've only ever lost both shoes." He shook his head in disbelief. "Then I wondered whether it might have belonged to this dirty old guy who I saw in the yard last night. He asked me whether Billy still lived in his house. I mean, everybody knows Billy lives in the house he was born in. This guy didn't seem very smart. Though he did look a lot like Billy."

I thought it better not to alert him to their relationship.

He heaved himself up to sit on the draining board, but I didn't dare scold him for fear of disrupting his flow.

"So I lobbed the shoe down the well, obviously, and then – " he raised his finger with professorial authority – "it was then that I realised that something wasn't right, because when the shoe landed in the well, there was no splash."

Still not entirely convinced that this wasn't an elaborate piece of mischief, I couldn't resist a joke.

"Well, you know the old saying, Tommy, about if a tree falls in the forest and no-one's there to hear it, does it make a sound? Perhaps it also works with wells."

I grinned feebly, but Tommy bulldozed on undeterred.

"But I was there to hear it, miss, so it should have done. And it landed with a thud, like on something solid. I thought at first that maybe Donald had just thrown a load of junk down there since I was chucking in stones last night, so I leaned over and looked down just to make sure he hadn't got rid of anything worth keeping, like old horseshoes or something. I collect old horseshoes." He brightened for a moment. "I've got loads in my bedroom. I thought they'd come in handy if I ever get a horse."

"So what did you find? Not a horse, surely?"

"This weird old man, all crumpled up with his head all over sideways."

I clapped my hands over my mouth to suppress a shriek. "So did you call the doctor?"

Tommy shook his head. "No point, Donald said. There wasn't anything a doctor could have done. He said the man was at such a funny angle, he must have broken his neck when he fell, and his body was all stiff too, so it was rigor – rigor something – rigorous exercise?"

He screwed up his face quizzically.

"*Rigor mortis.*"

"And did Donald recognise him?"

"Never seen him before in his life, he said."

I felt a chill spreading over me. "No, if it's who I think it is, Donald wasn't the landlord at The Bluebird last time this person was in the village."

I glanced across to Billy's table, where, poignantly, he was wrapping himself round tea and toast with his usual enthusiasm. I didn't want to be the one to break the news to him.

"You'd better get back up to the pub and tell Donald that Bob's already gone," I said, remembering Tommy's original mission. "He'll have to phone 999 and wait for the police to do their stuff. I expect they'll send a SOCO team – you know, scene of the crime officers – so there'll be no concreting today."

Tommy's eyes widened. "Wow, really? I can't wait to help them. Do you think they'll let me help them?"

I didn't answer. My head was spinning with the sudden realisation that Billy was probably the last person to have seen Bertie alive.

21 Well, Well

I was also mightily relieved to realise that Billy had spoken to Bertie after I did. Otherwise I might have been a murder suspect. After all, I had motives: my affection for Carol, and my ardent wish to see her live happily ever after with Ted, Becky and Arthur. And I had the opportunity: alone in the courtyard, unwitnessed, with Bertie. I also had the means: I may not have the strength of Wonder Woman, but as a fit, healthy twenty-five-year-old, I could easily have pushed a feeble, drunken old man backwards down a well.

As could Billy, strong of arm thanks to his twin employments of gardening and gravedigging. But did the brothers' mutual hatred really run that deep?

"I'll come back up there with you, Tommy," I said, wiping my hands on a tea towel and abandoning my post.

I dashed across to the trade counter to whisper to Hector a hint of what was transpiring. His jaw dropped as he listened to me.

"Yes, you go with him, sweetheart," he said in a low voice. "Go with Tommy and make sure he doesn't get himself into any serious trouble."

Did Hector think Tommy might somehow be involved? Much as he loved throwing things down the well, adding a full-grown man to his collection of missiles seemed unlikely. Unless Billy had put him up to it. It wouldn't be the first time that Billy had got Tommy to do his dirty work. Was that the favour that had earned Tommy his raffle ticket – pushing Bertie down the well?

I hesitated, clutching Hector's arm.

"What about the tearoom?" I gestured towards a couple of ladies just settling down at a newly vacated table.

"Don't worry, I'll call Becky." He pressed a speed dial code on his phone and put it to his ear. I didn't know he had Becky on speed dial.

But there was no time to fret at how easily I might be replaced. I followed Tommy to the door and up the High Street. Running to keep up with Tommy's long strides, I realised just how strong this wiry young boy had become.

In the courtyard, the village doctor was peering down the well beside Donald.

"The cops have gone from Hector's House, Donald, so you'll have to phone 999," Tommy was saying as I caught up with him. "And don't go disturbing the scene of the crime. There might be clues."

He pulled his magnifying glass out of his Parka pocket. The doctor straightened up and laid a firm but gentle hand on Tommy's arm.

"We'd better leave that to the experts, son. I'll put in a call now."

Tommy's shoulders sagged. "I'm only trying to help."

"I know, son," said the doctor. "But the best help you can give till the police get here is to try to remember exactly how you found the body. That will be very helpful indeed."

I was thankful to the doctor for his sensitivity.

Tommy perked up. "Shouldn't I have a lawyer present?"

"No-one's being accused of anything," said Donald. "We just need to piece together what we can, to give the police a head start finding out who did it and why. As you discovered the body, you're a very important witness."

Tommy straightened his shoulders proudly. "Yes, I suppose I am. That makes me sort of like a detective, doesn't it?"

The doctor nodded. "I suppose it does. Now, let's go inside and get our wits about us before the police get here. Donald, can you cover up the – er – the well in the meantime?"

While the doctor and Tommy returned to the bar, I helped Donald haul a sheet of plywood from the skip and position it across the top of the well's low wall. Then Donald placed a few of bricks on it hold it down. He glanced up at me sheepishly. "Am I overdoing it, Sophie?"

I shrugged. "I don't think he'll try to escape, if that's what you're worried about."

Poor Donald's face was pale with shock. After the euphoria the Valentine's Night success, this was the last thing he needed.

Gently I took his arm to steer him indoors. "Come on, Donald. You never know, when this gets in the local papers, it might bring lots of new customers up from Slate Green."

Donald groaned. "Oh God, the papers. That's all I need. Whatever will the brewery say?"

"Ker-ching," I said, and was glad to see him smile albeit briefly.

Once inside, we settled down with Tommy and the doctor round the table nearest the bar.

"You don't think they'll say it's all my fault, do you, Doc?" asked Donald. "Wretched health and safety. This is exactly why I've been wanting to get the well filled in. But I was more concerned about toddlers falling down it, not grown men. Honestly, you'd think someone his age would have more sense."

I bit my lip. "It was awfully dark out there last night, though, Donald."

All three swivelled round to stare at me.

"How do you know it was dark out there last night?"

"I... I heard a noise, and went out, and... and I saw the old man. I talked to him. He was alive and standing there large as life. I know it was the same man, I recognise him, even in the daylight. And I know who he is - was." I hesitated. "He was Billy Thompson's brother, Bertie."

They gasped.

"His older brother. He seemed a bit tipsy to me. But you know, old people don't see well at night. Joshua, next door to me, he has to use really bright lightbulbs to see properly. Maybe Bertie just tripped."

"But that's what the wall is for," said Donald. "That little wall around the well. To stop people falling down it. It's not like it was a concealed mineshaft, with no outward clues. You can't fall down a well, just like that."

"You might if you were a bit drunk," I said uncertainly.

Tommy thumped his hand down on the table, making us all jump.

"You could if someone pushed you," he said, turning pale. "And I can think of someone who might have pushed Bertie down the well."

196

22 Slow Motion

"Tommy Crowe, you promised me you wouldn't tell no-one about seeing my brother here last night." A vein on Billy's forehead was pulsing hard enough to worry me. "I thought you and me was friends. I said you could only have my raffle ticket if you didn't tell no-one about meeting him."

This was hardly the reaction I'd expected Billy to have to the news of his brother's death. Seeing the pub door open on his way home from Hector's House, he had strolled in on the off-chance of an early pint.

Tommy grimaced. "You never told me he was your brother. I'm sorry, Billy, I really am. But it's too late now to give you back your raffle ticket, because we won the hamper, and Sina and me have eaten all the chocolates, and my mum's drunk all the champagne. So unless you want us to sick them all up again –"

Billy snarled and turned away. I hated seeing these two unlikely but loyal friends torn apart by this awful discovery, when Tommy might have been a comfort to the old man in his time of need. Billy's eyes were filling with tears. He turned to me in appeal. "I know I've said some harsh things about Bertie in the past, but he was my brother. Even if he did say some awful things about Carol last night, still shameless after all these years. What decent man wouldn't have lain a few punches on his chest to try to shut him up? But he was my only surviving brother, my only living flesh and blood. I wouldn't have it in me to kill the old bugger."

"Your only living relative, apart from all the other people in the village you're related to," said the doctor gently, the corner of his mouth twitching in amusement.

Billy scowled again. "Well, you knows what I mean. The only close member of my family that's left. My only sibling. Don't that count for nothing these days?"

Tommy leaned over to whisper to me. "Most murderers know their victims personally." I wished he hadn't committed so much of his detective book to memory. I bet he wasn't as good with French verbs and algebraic formulae.

"But why would anyone think I'd murder my own brother? We weren't no Cain and Abel." Bertie's voice was plaintive. "And why now? If I'd wanted to kill him, I could have done so long before now. Not that I ever bested Bertie in a fight when we were youngsters, and I didn't intend to start now. It must have been someone else, but who would do such a thing?"

"Don't answer that, Tommy," I said quickly. "Let's leave it to the real police to ask the questions."

I pulled the tearoom order pad and a pencil out of my pocket, and a pencil, and started to make a note of the sequence of events from the night before.

Carol had come in from the courtyard after me, claiming Bertie had stood her up. Supposing Ted had somehow found out about it? Becky might have tipped him off, feeling vengeful towards her father and wanting something better for her mum. Those strong baker's hands would have no trouble thrusting a feeble old man down a hole in the ground.

Donald looked at his watch and got up from the table. "I'd better tell the concrete men to come back another time." He headed for the door.

Of course, I only had Carol's word for it that she hadn't seen Bertie when I bumped into her outside the Gents'. She could easily have pushed Bertie down the well before she came through the side door. I thought she seemed a little over-excited for someone who had only come to the pub to supervise a prize draw. That was before she'd spotted Ted there waiting for her.

I looked sideways at Tommy, currently absorbed by dismantling a sugar lump grain by grain.

Donald returned, shaking his head. "They said they've got to charge me full whack for this mix. This courtyard is going to cost me a fortune." He sighed. "Why did this have to happen on our busiest night of the year? The only one when there wasn't a regular trickle of smokers out to the courtyard? Otherwise someone would have spotted what was going on and stopped it." He locked his eyes on mine. "If it hadn't been for your Valentine's Dinner, we might have saved the poor old soul."

I gasped at the injustice. "It wasn't MY Valentine's Dinner."

"I don't know why you two are getting so aerated about concrete and Valentine's nonsense," said Billy, his voice cracking as he spoke. "It's not looking good for me, is it? I mean, no-one seems to have seen him after I did. And I swear on our mother's grave, I left him alive."

"Perhaps he jumped down the well," said Tommy brightly. "I mean, it's the sort of thing a person might do."

Donald put his hand over his mouth to cover a laugh. "It might be the sort of thing you would do, you crazy child," he said, "but not the average old man on a dark night."

"From what I saw of Bertie, I don't think he would have been capable of jumping," I said. "Staggering, perhaps."

"But over a wall?" asked Donald. "Not unless somebody pushed him over it."

"You mean, did he fall or was he pushed?" I said. "Perhaps we'll never know. Not unless you've got a hidden camera out there."

"But of course I have." Donald clapped a hand to his forehead. "CCTV. It's very low resolution, and a bit clapped out, but it might help. Quick, let's take a look before the police get here."

"Might you hide the evidence if it shows Billy killed him, then?" asked Tommy, sounding like he thought it was a genuine possibility. "You mustn't do that, Donald. That would be wrong."

"Of course not," said Donald, marching across to the bar and lifting the flap. "Come on, you can all come and witness it if you like, to make sure I don't tamper with the evidence."

Tommy, the doctor and I got to our feet and followed Donald, leaving Billy sitting with his head in his hands.

"The camera automatically downloads onto my PC at midnight every night, so yesterday's footage will be on here already," said Donald, punching 6pm on 14 February into the search box, then setting it to run on fast forward.

There were two screens side by side showing footage from two separate cameras, one pointing from the rear wall of the pub towards the well, the other positioned above the side door and pointing down the alley.

"I'm in it quite a lot, aren't I, Donald?" said Tommy, admiring the speeded-up footage of him lobbing stone after stone down the well. I hoped Donald hadn't been intending to keep that bit of wall.

Donald ignored him. "Here, now we're getting somewhere. It's too dark to see the details clearly, but that's obviously you, Sophie, having a chat with Bertie, and very wisely keeping your distance from him."

After I'd gone back up the alley and disappeared inside the pub, we saw Bertie lurking by the well on his own for a bit, stumbling about, clapping his arms around himself for warmth.

"He didn't have a very thick coat on for such a cold night," said the doctor. "He could well have been verging on hypothermia if he'd been out there too long at his age."

Then, the footage still on fast-forward, Billy emerged into the alley and made straight for Bertie. There were no brotherly hugs of welcome after their decades of separation. Instead there followed agitated, jerky movements of heads and arms, as they engaged in what looked like a ferocious row. They kept their distance from each other until Billy took a step forward to strike his brother, smacking him, open fisted, on the chest in anger, once, twice, three times, before turning on his heel and marching away from him.

We held our breath as Billy departed, leaving Bertie stood there, wobbling slightly, then a bit more, and more and more, like the final skittle reluctant to allow a player a strike. Finally gravity got the better of him, and he tumbled, arms and legs flailing, dislodging a shoe on the low wall as he tipped over backwards at an awkward angle. When he bashed his head on the far side of the well, we all flinched.

"That must have been the moment of death," said the doctor quietly.

Then Bertie disappeared completely down the well.

We were silent as Donald rewound those last few moments, making Bertie reappear, spookily, like a rabbit from a magician's hat.

"That's clever," said Tommy appreciatively.

This time when Donald clicked play, he let the film run in real time.

"Bertie must have cried out when he fell," said the doctor. "So why didn't Billy stop to help him?"

"Billy," I said slowly, feeling relief starting to wash over me, "Billy forgot to put his hearing aids in last night. He was on his way back down the passage by the time that Bertie lost his footing. He couldn't possibly have heard."

I pointed at the screen as Donald reran the footage once more.

"Look, if he had heard it, he would have reacted. He'd have jumped, or turned round, instinctively, even if he chose not to go to his aid. But look at him, he just keeps walking. He plainly hasn't heard a thing."

Donald rewound to show the brothers arguing beside the well again, and this time we could see plainly that the push that Billy had given him hadn't been of murderous intent. All he'd done was set his brother a little off balance. The physical frailty inflicted by Bertie's dissolute, drunken life had done the rest, and in the shadow of the cottage in which the brothers had been born, Bertie Thompson had tumbled to his accidental death.

The bar flap clattered behind us, and we turned to see Billy standing, pale and helpless, to await our verdict.

"Find anything worth seeing?"

"It was an accident, Billy, just a very unfortunate accident," said the doctor slowly. "Of that we can be absolutely sure."

"Pardon?" said Billy. "Speak up, I can't hear you if you're going to whisper."

I turned to the doctor and smiled. "I rest my case."

By the time the police had come and gone, and the ambulance had taken Bertie's body away to the morgue, it was past lunchtime. I thought I'd better head back to Hector's House. I hoped he had been missing me, in spite of the ease with which he'd fielded Becky as a substitute.

The shop was much quieter than when I'd left. Hector, seeing me as I pushed the door open, looked up anxiously.

"Everything ok up there, Sophie?"

I nodded. "Sort of."

He pointed to the central display table, where gaps like missing teeth had appeared where copies of *The Girl with Forget-Me-Not Eyes* had once been piled high.

"Look at that! We're sold out! We've sold every last copy." He grinned. "I can see the headlines in next month's *Bookseller*, can't you, Sophie? 'Minty's Minting It'. And it'll all be down to you."

"Lovely," I said weakly, although I meant it. "But what I really need now is a nice cup of tea."

If you enjoyed reading this book,
you might like to spread the word to other readers
by leaving a brief review online —
or just tell your friends!
Thank you.

For the latest information about
Debbie Young's books and events,
visit her Writing Life website,
where you may also like to join
her free Readers' Club:
www.authordebbieyoung.com

Acknowledgements

Enormous thanks to all the people who have helped make this a better book:

- Orna Ross for her wise and sensitive mentoring
- Novelists Lucienne Boyce and Belinda Pollard for their insightful and tactful beta reading
- Alison Jack, my editor, always patient, capable, and dependable
- Rachel Lawston of Lawston Design for another wonderful book cover design
- Zoe Gooding of Zedolus Proofreading for peace of mind
- My friend Jacky Taylor for her entertaining and useful observations about the hands of bakers
- My daughter Laura for reminding me of the Mark Twain cited at the start of the book
- Lorna Ferguson, for suggesting an appropriate book for Edward Munro to read
- Elizabeth Tebby Germaine for alerting me to the history of the nursery rhyme Ding Dong Dell
- Sharon, Alex and Natasha Gray for their advice on reference books about saints

I hope readers concerned about Sophie's literary ignorance in the first three books in the series may be heartened by her progress in this book, even if she doesn't always get her references quite right. Working in a bookshop is making her absorb knowledge and culture almost by osmosis. Ah, the power of the traditional independent bookshop, and of the humble, old-fashioned book in our high-tech age!

Debbie Young

Also by Debbie Young

Sophie Sayers Village Mysteries
Best Murder in Show (1)
Trick or Murder? (2)
Murder in the Manger (3)
Coming soon:
Springtime for Murder (5)
Murder Your Darlings (6)
School's Out for Summer (7)

Short Story Collections
Marry in Haste
Quick Change
Stocking Fillers

Essay Collections
All Part of the Charm:
　　A Modern Memoir of English Village Life
Young By Name:
　　Whimsical Columns from the Tetbury Advertiser

More
Sophie Sayers
Village Mysteries

Coming Soon:
Springtime for Murder

(Sophie Sayers Village Mysteries #5)

When Sophie finds an Easter bunny as big as herself left for dead in an open grave, she is drawn into a local family feud with dangerous implications for her friends and neighbours in the Cotswold village of Wendlebury Barrow.

Join Sophie, her boyfriend, the village bookseller Hector Munro, and their irrepressible teenage sidekick Tommy Crowe as they to try to track down the killer who is threatening to wipe out a village dynasty.

To be published in paperback and ebook
(September 2018)

Best Murder in Show
(Sophie Sayers Village Mysteries #1)

When Sophie Sayers inherits a cottage in a sleepy Cotswold village, she's hoping for a quieter life than the one she's running away from. What she gets instead is a dead body on a carnival float, and an extraordinary assortment of suspects.

Is the enigmatic bookseller Hector Munro all he seems? And what about the over-friendly neighbour who brings her jars of honey? Not to mention the eccentric village shopkeeper, show committee, writers' group and drama club, all suspiciously keen to welcome her to their midst.

For fans of cosy mysteries everywhere, *Best Murder in Show* will make you laugh out loud at the idiosyncrasies of English country life and rack your brains to discover the murderer before Sophie can.

"A cracking example of cosy crime" – Katie Fforde

Available in paperback and ebook
ISBN 978-1-911223-13-9 (paperback)
ISBN 978-1-911223-14-6 (ebook)

Trick or Murder?
(Sophie Sayers Village Mysteries #2)

Just when Sophie Sayers is starting to feel at home in the Cotswold village of Wendlebury Barrow, a fierce new vicar arrives, quickly offending her and everyone else he meets.

Banning the villagers' Halloween celebrations seems the last straw, particularly when instead he revives the old English Guy Fawkes' tradition with a bonfire piled high with sinister effigies.

And what dark secret is he hiding about her boss, the beguiling bookseller Hector Munro? Whose body is that outside the village bookshop? Not to mention the one buried beneath the vicar's bonfire.

For fans of cosy mysteries everywhere, Sophie's second adventure will have you laughing out loud as you try to solve the mystery before she does, in the company of engaging new characters, as well as familiar favourites from Best Murder in Show.

"Debbie Young delves into the awkwardness
of human nature in a deft and funny way:
Miss Marple meets Bridget Jones."
Belinda Pollard, *Wild Crimes series*

Available in paperback and ebook
ISBN 978-1-911223-20-7 (paperback)
ISBN 978-1-911223-19-1 (ebook)

Murder in the Manger
(Sophie Sayers Village Mysteries #3)

When Sophie Sayers' plans for a cosy English country Christmas are interrupted by the arrival of her ex-boyfriend, her troubles are only just beginning. Before long, the whole village stands accused of murder.

Damian says he's come to direct the village nativity play, but Sophie thinks he's up to no good. What are those noises coming from his van? Who is the stranger lurking in the shadows? And whose baby, abandoned in the manger, disappears in plain sight?

Enjoy the fun of a traditional Christmas festive season with echoes of Dickens' A Christmas Carol *as Sophie seeks a happy ending for her latest village mystery – and her new romance with charming local bookseller Hector Munro.*

> *"The funniest opening line in a novel, period.*
> *I can't get enough of the*
> *Sophie Sayers Village Mystery series.*
> *Wendy H Jones,*
> *author of DI Shona McKenzie thrillers*

Available in paperback and ebook
ISBN 978-1-911223-22-1 (paperback)
ISBN 978-1-911223-21-4 (ebook)

Printed in Great Britain
by Amazon